A DAY ON THE RIVER

A HODGKISS MYSTERY

XXXV

PETER SINCLAIR

Published in Australia by Peter Sinclair
First published in Australia 2022
Copyright © Peter Sinclair 2022
Cover design, typesetting: WorkingType Studio

A Day on the River: A Hodgkiss Mystery
Volume XXXV

ISBN: 978-0-6455762-4-5

Sinclair, Peter

pp244

About the author

Peter Sinclair has spent most of his working life writing. He began reporting courts and councils in rural Orange (NSW) in the late 1950s then worked briefly for *The Sydney Daily Telegraph* where, because of his fluent shorthand, he was sentenced first to report local councils then banished to the Coroner's Court.

He'd had enough of sudden death and murder when opportunity knocked and he joined the staff of a new, large weekly paper in Sydney's northern suburbs, *The North Shore Times* where he was soon reporting councils again.

In 1965, he climbed over the journalistic fence to work as press secretary for a succession of NSW cabinet ministers (both Liberal and Labor) until 1991. Since then, he has made guest reappearances to help out in the PR sections of government departments.

His absorbing hobby is playing the piano. He has made

a number of CDs in very limited editions. The titles tell it all: Peter Murders Mozart, Wrecks Rachmaninoff and Desecrates Debussy. He says he gives them away to people he doesn't like!

He has been married to Margaret for fifty-seven years and they have two sons; Sam, who is married to Carolyn with one son, Harry, 18, and Patrick who is married to Beejai with twin boys, Jackson and Zachary, aged 13.

Author Note

Every now and then I type 'The Hodgkiss Mysteries' into Google to see how the old fellow is being accepted.

At first he was to be found only in a couple of local libraries and bookshops.

Now he appears to be everywhere ... in many different countries.

Hodgkiss is available in lands where they speak French, German, Japanese and Swedish among other tongues, and in alphabets I do not recognise. Of course not in translation.

For some reason he seems to be particularly popular in some southern states of the US. Libraries in California, Texas and Arizona offer their readers a large selection of his adventures.

It is encouraging to think that people out there are reading about him.

For Margaret

For James Connaught the operation to replace his right knee was one of the most traumatic experiences of his life.

It had all started as a niggling pain six months ago. Very soon the pain became so severe that James visited his general practitioner who referred him to another doctor who had injected his knee with something that gave almost instant relief.

But the doctor warned that the relief would be only temporary, and in less than a month the pain returned, now more severe than ever. So James returned to his GP who this time referred him to a specialist surgeon.

The surgeon explained that James must chose between a knee replacement operation or continuing pain which would only get worse as bone ground upon bone every time he put weight on the leg.

The surgeon, a short, jolly man, sat at his desk and tapped on his computer as James described his symptoms and the history of his problem.

Arrangements were made and a date was set six weeks hence for the operation.

The surgeon mentioned a figure for the operation which did not include the fee for the anesthetist who would bill him separately.

The sum should be paid in full in the week before the operation.

James told the surgeon that his credit card would not cover such a large amount and asked if cash would be all right.

For the first time the man looked up from his screen, surprised. He nodded. 'Yes,' he said.

On the day before the operation the hospital rang to say that James should be there at six in the morning and gave directions where to come.

James was on time, as he was usually for any appointment, and the process began.

He was taken to a bed in a ward with three other men. Curtains were drawn around the bed as he undressed and he placed all his clothes and other possessions in a large drawstring bag. Then he put on a thin gown that was secured at the rear with two ribbons which he was unable to tie without the assistance of a nurse.

He lay in the bed, cold and anxious.

He had not been there long when a short man in a dark suit pushed through the curtains. The anaesthetist. The man introduced himself as Dr Fine, mentioned the amount of his fee, took James' pulse and departed without another word.

About an hour later two nurses came. One of them

shaved his right leg above the knee, while the other drew on his thigh in indelible marker pen an arrow pointing down to the knee. James joked about it, uneasily.

Soon a wardsman came and wheeled his bed through a maze of corridors to a room outside the operating theatre.

When his surgeon arrived, his mask in place, James did not at first know him.

At last he was wheeled into the operating theatre where he lay, turned to one side, looking through the bars of the raised side of the hospital bed.

Is this it, he thought. Is this how it all ends ... my last glimpse of the world.

Then a needle slipped into his arm and he slept.

When he woke he was in the same bed in a curtained area. There was a nurse standing beside him.

His memory of those first hours was confused. He recalled being given a device to hold. He could press the button to relieve pain.

Suspecting that it contained some powerful opiate James decided to make sparing use of the button.

Then to his surprise that same afternoon he was taken from his bed, given a pair of crutches and told to walk up and down the corridor outside his room.

After this the daily regime became fairly predictable. Early wakening alone in a single room. Breakfast, a tasteless meal of porridge and tea and toast, then exercise.

He saw the surgeon only twice during the week he was at the hospital and both visits were brief. The wound, bandaged and wrapped in some plastic substance, was examined and pronounced satisfactory.

After the week was up he was transferred by ambulance to a hospital nearby which specialised in the rehabilitation of those who had undergone the replacement of various body parts.

It was there, at the Lady Anderson Memorial Hospital, that James Connaught met William Berger.

*　　*　　*

Later, when they compared notes, James discovered that William had undergone an experience very similar to his own; the painful knee; the jolly surgeon, the near-invisible anesthetist and the crushing financial cost of the whole operation ... and that cost was by no means the end as both faced the further cost of their rehabilitation.

Throughout their daily contacts during rehabilitation exercises there seemed to be an unspoken acknowledgment that once they were deemed safe to be discharged that the two probably would never meet again, although they lived in nearby suburbs.

The exercises occupied an hour in the morning and another in the afternoon. Those who oversaw their efforts were mostly young women who insisted that they adhere strictly to every detail of their prescribed routines which concentrated on flexibility and balance. All were extremely painful at first.

But soon, as their rehabilitation progressed, they often found themselves pedaling energetically on adjoining exercise bicycles.

It was during these sessions, when the pain was no longer intrusive, that rational thought and conversation became possible.

Then the pandemic arrived. It changed everything.

'Experts' predicted that hundreds of thousands would die and governments around the country took fright and locked the population in its homes for months at a time.

In their hospital little changed except face masks were worn much of the time and visits were suspended.

Pedaling side by side on exercise bikes William learned that James was married to Phyllis whose main ambition in life, according to James, was to lose the family's money as quickly as possible in the poker machines at a local RSL club. The advent of the virus had in no way restricted her ambition because as soon as the club's gaming room was closed Phyllis simply transferred to the many forms of online gambling offered on her smart phone.

So her loses were continuing, now at a faster rate than ever.

James learned that William and his wife, Esther, were joint managers of three flourish coffee shops in nearby suburbs.

But the army of coffee lovers, who each day ventured out to eat at one or other of the city's tens of thousands of cafes, found that the new rules, imposed due to the virus, allowed them only to take away their coffee and food. No more could they sit down to a Big Breakkie or enjoy their coffee in comfort with a croissant or a friand and chat with a friend.

But the cafe society survived … just.

Many cafe staff, cooks, waiters and baristas, caught the virus and stayed away from work for weeks at a time.

Many cafes closed their doors simply through lack of staff to serve.

While the owners of these cafes were well aware of these problems they still demanded their rents, and William's landlord, Cory Wisdom, was one of these.

While governments gave employers money to pay staff in order to keep the economy running this did not always work as intended.

When Cory Wisdom received the government money none of it was passed on to enable William and Esther to pay their staff.

Wisdom put the government's money in his own pocket, leaving those for whom it was intended, to fend for themselves.

William and Esther were now using the last of their savings to pay their staff in an effort to survive the virus.

Bankruptcy threatened.

*   *   *

James Connaught had completely forgotten about William Berger when the name appeared on the screen of his phone.

For a while they chatted about how well their knees had

healed. They spoke without exaggeration of how well they could walk now; how they were free of pain; how pleased they were with their outcomes.

Then James asked how were the three cafes surviving. Since William had made no secret of the problems he and his wife Esther were experiencing in surviving the pandemic, it was natural that James should ask.

William told him how Corey Wisdom had ignored the government's appeals to landlords to treat tenants leniently to enable them to survive the pandemic; how Wisdom had ignored his plea for time to pay back rent; how Wisdom had told him that it was not up to any government to interfere in private legal arrangements and that William must meet his commitments or hand over the cafes to more competent and innovative managers.

William had calculated that he and Esther had enough money put aside to pay rent and wages for another two weeks if business did not improve, something that could not happen unless 'lock-down' orders were lifted.

But there was no sign of that happening soon.

'So, short of a miracle we'll be out of business any day now. Gone ... broke ... and all on account of that greedy bastard.'

'Well, I've got problems too, as you know,' said James. 'The wife's gambling ... not as bad as yours, I know, but maybe I can help you or we can help each other. Perhaps we should meet and talk things over.'

William muttered agreement. 'OK. But what have you got in mind?'

'Not on the phone,' said James.

They arranged to meet the following week at a nearby coffee shop.

James arrived first and was standing beside his car, parked at an angle outside Frendz Cafe in West Lillimoor, when William arrived.

James lowered his face-mask. 'What will it be, William?' he asked. reaching around for his wallet. 'My shout,' he added.

'I suppose we'll have to sit in one of the cars, will we?' said William nodding towards the signs on the tables that said No Table Service.

'There's a park opposite,' said James. 'We could sit there,' he said as he headed towards the service hatch.

William nodded agreement and crossed the road to a well-kept children's playground. He sat on an old uncomfortable bench-seat and waited.

Soon James was hurrying across the road, a cardboard tray containing two Styrofoam beakers in one hand and a paper bag in the other.

'I hope you like friands,' said James, taking his seat beside William, but not too close.

William took a friand from the bag and the two of them began eating.

Their conversation soon turned to the virus and its ill-effects upon so many aspects of daily life.

William nodded towards the cafe across the road. 'It doesn't hit everyone the same, you know,' he said. 'The fellow who runs that place, I know him. He's surviving OK because most of his business is still turning up. All locals and tradies, all happy to take-away. It doesn't make a lot of difference to him. Lucky guy.'

James sipped his coffee cautiously. 'What about you? Your landlord still refusing to cut you any slack?'

'Man's a bastard,' said William with feeling. 'He takes the money the government gives him to pay wages so people can keep their jobs, and what does he do ... he trousers the lot. Of course we couldn't keep paying the staff out of our own pocket. We did for as long as possible hoping the government would let us open up. But it never happened. We're finished now. I closed the doors last week. We're broke ... Esther and I.

'And what about you?' William asked. 'Is Phyllis still gambling? I suppose the club's still closed, is it?'

James nodded. 'The gaming room's locked up but that hasn't stopped her. Now she's playing on the internet ... on her iPad. It's worse. She loses more than ever ... and faster. I've tried everything ... hiding the iPad ... threatening her ... trying to get her to join up to one of those gambling anonymous groups ... everything I can think of.'

William sipped his coffee. 'Thought of everything short of murder, have you, eh?'

James put down his friand and looked up. He smiled. 'Actually that's what I want to talk to you about. Murder.'

*   *   *

'Murder.' William repeated the word cautiously ... unbelieving. 'You can't be serious.' Then: 'Who? Murder Wisdom you mean?'

James nodded. 'Of course. Or is there someone else you'd like to see dead?'

William shook his head. 'Of course not. But I could never do it ... much as I'd like to I couldn't. I'd never have the nerve. Besides, I can't stand violence ... or the sight of blood ... even my own.'

'But people can die non-violent deaths,' said James ... 'with no blood spilled.'

William continued to shake his head. 'Yes, maybe so, but I still couldn't do it. I know it.'

'But that's the beauty of it ... you wouldn't have to do it. I'd do it for you.'

'You? Why would you do it? You don't even know him.'

James laughed. 'What difference does that make. It probably makes it easier.'

'But why? There must be a reason.'

'Of course there's a reason. I'd kill him and you'd kill Phyllis, because death is the only thing that's ever going to stop her gambling.'

William held up a hand. 'No way. That's the oldest trick in the book. In fact books have been written about it ... they've made movies about it. The police would be onto us in no time.'

James shook his head. 'Not necessarily. You and me ... we hardly know each other. Our paths crossed in that hospital

… in rehab … for just a week. Even if they found out … so what?'

William paused. 'Maybe. But to actual kill someone … I couldn't do it. Not in cold blood. Not even in hot blood … not even Wisdom …much as I despise him and much as he'd deserve it'

'But you wouldn't be killing Wisdom. You'd be killing Phyllis, my wife … a complete stranger. Besides it depends on *how* you do it, surely,' said James, not prepared to give up. 'You don't have to be involved … not personally. You don't have to do it with your own bare hands.'

'Poison you mean?' William asked. 'Something like that.'

'Yes. Poison. Or too many sleeping pills … or an accident … in the car.'

'Tamper with the brakes or the steering, you mean? I wouldn't know how to go about it.'

'Really? I don't think it would be all that difficult.'

'And poison … what poison. Where would I get it? How much do you use? How would I get her to take it? Don't you have to sign your name to buy it in the first place?'

'That's in detective stories,' said James. 'You might have to sign your name if you go to a chemist to get arsenic or cyanide or something like that. But there're plenty of deadly poisons you can buy over the counter at any hardware shop … rat poison … that kind of thing.'

'Maybe, but they'd taste awful, wouldn't they?

'She'd know as soon as she tasted it. Have you ever done it …. killed someone?'

James shook his head. 'No. Never. Never wanted to until now.'

'So why don't you just get on and do it yourself ... kill your wife?'

'I'd never get away with it,' said James. 'Everyone knows that the husband's the first person the police suspect. Everybody ... all our friends know about Phyls' problem. They know we don't get on any more because of it. And some of them, her friends, they'd be happy to talk to the police. They'd volunteer. They wouldn't have to be asked.'

William nodded. 'So you want me to do it ... kill your wife, and you'd see to Corey Wisdom? Is that what you're saying?'

James nodded. 'That's it ... exactly. What do you say?' He held up a hand. 'No. I don't want an answer straight away. Just promise me that you'll think about it. Right?'

*　　*　　*

The premises of the Buccaneer's Bay Cruising Club was an unpretentious affair; a single storey of brick with a modest marina nearby on the riverfront to accommodate members' boats.

Because of its superb location the club's management committee regularly received and refused offers to purchase. A more prestigious club, The Victor Amory Memorial Yacht Club, half a kilometre up the river, had made several offers without success.

Not that the Cruising Club was flush with funds. Because

the management always kept members' fees to the barest minimum, maintenance around the building sometimes suffered.

The fact that several of the members were tradesmen who gave their time and expertise free of charge ensured that the building survived in serviceable condition.

One of these members, Gordon Tracey, dressed smartly in a blue jacket, white shirt, shorts and a captain's cap, was pacing the wide verandah at the front of the clubhouse, frequently glancing at the large automatic watch strapped to his right wrist.

His wife, Nola, was sitting on a swing seat, watching him with an amused smile. She wore only a midriff top and short shorts to show long tanned legs crossed at the knee, feet bare.

'You didn't really think they'd be on time, did you?' she asked. When he said nothing she continued. 'People like them are never on time They don't care how long they make you wait. You might as well come and sit down.'

But Gordon continued pacing. 'They'll be here any minute,' he said.

Nola shook her head. 'Actually I'm surprised he agreed to come at all. He must know you're going to put the bite on him.'

Gordon nodded. 'Very likely.'

'And you don't really think that he's going to give you anything, surely.'

Gordon shrugged. 'Who knows. He might. It's certainly worth the try anyway. His father was a decent old fellow.'

Nola looked up in amazement. 'A decent old fellow. Is that what you think of him? He used you as slave labour around that huge old house of his for years. Called you up any time of the day or night if any little thing went wrong and off you'd run at the drop of a hat to fix whatever it was; a blocked toilet, fix the heating, even change a light bulb because he said he was too old to get up a ladder ... and you were almost as old as him. A decent old fellow! If he was a decent old fellow he would have given you back the money you put out on those dud shares he sold you on. Make your fortune, he said. Then what does he do ... he dies the very day they come on the market for a huge loss.'

Gordon stopped his pacing and turned. 'The shock killed him, That's what James thinks. I suppose he could be right.'

'What does it matter what killed him. He's gone and now it's up to this James, who you hardly even know, to do the right thing. I'm not holding my breath. If he doesn't come good big-time we're going to lose everything ... the boat, the semi ... the lot. Everything we've worked for.'

Gordon nodded and glanced at his watch again.

*   *   *

In fact James and Phyllis Connaught were still more than ten minutes away from the club.

'Don't fret about it, James,' said Phyllis. 'They won't mind waiting. They're probably used to it.'

'Why should they be used to waiting?' said James,

frowning over the steering wheel. 'You don't like to be kept waiting, do you? You're the first to complain.'

Phyllis ignored the question. 'You know what this is all about, don't you, James … this invitation to go out on their looooverly boat? It's about money. This Gordon fellow is going to ask you to make up the money he lost on those shares your father told him to buy.'

James shook his head. 'No. I doubt if he'd do that. He knew shares are always a gamble. He knew he was taking a risk when he bought them. Dad didn't give any sort of promise or guarantee … and he lost money on them too … and so did we.'

'Yes, but we didn't go in big like this Gordon fellow. I heard your father talking to him on the phone the day before the shares came on the market. When he hung up he told me that he wished he hadn't told him about them because he'd put everything he had into the shares … and he'd even borrowed to buy more. Your Dad said Gordon would be ruined if they didn't come on the market strongly … and we all know how badly wrong that went. Still, that's the way it works … or not.'

'You don't sound exactly sorry for them,' said James pressing down the left-turn indicator .

'Sorry for them! Why on earth should I feel sorry for them? He was just plain greedy.'

'He was taking Dad's advice don't forget. He'd taken it in the past and it was always good.'

'Then he'd already made good money in the past on your father's say-so. Now he's lost some. Let him live with it.'

15

'You're a hard woman Phyl. And why on earth did you have to wear all your best gear today … I thought you were going to get the tiara out.'

'And why on earth shouldn't I wear a few of my good things sometimes. You never take me anywhere I can wear anything decent. When was the last time I had an excuse to dress up a bit?'

'You call that dressing up a bit? Going out on a boat is hardly the right occasion to deck yourself out like that. What if there's a storm and it gets rough. You could lose the lot over the side.'

Phyllis shook her head, smiling. 'I don't think so, James. But not to worry. They're all insured.' Then, 'Look. Is that the place up ahead there. Not much of a club if you ask me.'

'Yes, that's it. And there's Gordon and Nola waiting on the verandah,' said James as he turned in and drove towards the visitor parking area at the side of the clubhouse.

*   *   *

'My God, Gordon,' said Nola, as Phyllis stepped out of the car. 'Just look at what's arrived, will you. She can't be serious. Even high heels. Must think she's going to a cocktail party.'

'Keep it down a bit,' Gordon hissed. 'She might hear you.'

But Phyllis had heard. Smart bitch, she thought. I'll teach her thing or two before the day's out.

Gordon hurried across to greet his guests, waving for Nola to follow him.

Phyllis saw her husband run an interested glance over Nola. Best keep an eye on that, she thought.

When the introductions had been made Gordon said; 'I'm afraid the first thing we have to do is to sign you both in the visitors' book. Rules, you know. Its just in the foyer.'

In the foyer Phyllis looked around at some peeling paint on the wall and a dark stain in one corner of the ceiling.

Seeing her glance Gordon explained. 'Bit of rain came in during that last downpour. The committee's working on it now.'

'Don't you have a painter or two among your members?' Phyllis asked. 'Or perhaps you could turn one of your many practical talents to the task, Gordon, and save the club a few dollars.'

Before Gordon could answer Nola said; 'We've found that having practical talents is not always appreciated.'

Gordon cringed. If Nola kept this going their chances of James giving them a financial hand would be nil.

He said. 'I'd say a few of us will finish up doing the job. The committee feels its got to go through the motions of calling for tenders etcetra etcetra. It's probably in the constitution or something,' he ended lamely.

When James and Phyllis had signed their names and addresses in the rather tatty visitors' book and Nola had countersigned in the next column, Gordon suggested: 'Why don't we have a little look around, although there's not that much to see really.'

The club's only bar was not a cheerful place although

it was big enough. It ran across the entire width of the building and gave a view over the river. Two ancient poker machines stood side by side in a neglected niche next to the door to the toilets.

The room's only other occupant, the barman, an elderly, slow-moving man, looked up, surprised.

Gordon explained; 'This is Albert,' he said avoiding a formal introduction. 'Albert is something of an institution around here. He's been with the club almost from the day we opened. I couldn't tell you how long ago that was.'

If anyone had wanted to calculate the length of Albert's service they could have glanced at one of the wooden plaques on the walls around the room that recorded the names of club champions in various categories of boating achievement and officebearers of the club going back to the year of the club's foundation.

Albert, now approaching his seventieth birthday, looked up when the group appeared at the door to the bar. Not much trade there, he thought. The couple with Gordon and Nola …they don't look like big tippers anyway, he decided, although the woman had more jewellery around her person than the club was worth, which Albert knew was very little.

He was on friendly terms with the club manager, the only other employee on the permanent pay roll. The manager, Phillip Spence, had been on the books for almost as long as Albert and there were very few secrets between the two.

During their conversations when Phillip came to the bar for a break from his labours, they would usually touch on the subject of the club's viability ... a question that gave them both cause for concern since both knew that a bankrupt club may not be in a position to pay their entitlements in full or even at all.

But Phillip's latest report to Albert was that they were likely to be still in work to the end of the year at least. Things with the bank were not yet too dire to be of immediate concern.

Albert noticed the look of disdain that passed across the face of the heavily-bejewel lady as she stood at the bar door, taking in the room.

The woman walked across to one of the laminate-topped tables in a corner of the bar. She ran a finger across the surface, inspected the finger and wrinkled her nose in disapproval. She turned and said something to the man who Albert assumed was her husband.

Doesn't think much of us, that one, Albert thought. I wonder why Gordon bothered to bring her here. Surely she's not going out on the river dressed up like that. If she fell over the side she'd go straight to the bottom.

Albert had a lot of time for Gordon and Nola. Gordon was a good steady club man. Pulled his weight around the place. Did odd jobs without complaining. Kept a very nice boat. And Nola? Well, she was very easy on the eye, that lady. And most of the the men around the club had noticed it too. At times he thought that she got rather too friendly with one or two of the members and that sometimes caused a bit of bother. But what do you expect when you let ladies in as members as the club had decided to do ten years ago. That was the only time he had seen a serous division of opinion among the membership.

But on balance Albert thought the decision had worked well although the women had not proved the financial boon the management had hoped for. 'It's always the ladies who play the pokies,' Phillip had told a meeting of members before the vote was taken. 'They can't stay away from them.'

But he had been wrong. The influx of women members had made a liar of him. They had ignored the two tired, dusty machines.

Seeing that his guests showed little interest in the bar Gordon decide to hasten what he now feared would be an embarrassing and unproductive day.

'A drink before we go?' he asked, in no doubt about what the answer would be.

'What? Drink before we go out on the boat,' said Phyllis, in the tone of one who can scarcely believe her ears. 'I really don't think that's such a very good idea, do you James?'

James, of course, agreed although Gordon was half way to the bar, wallet in hand.

'Very well,' said Gordon, happy to return the wallet to his jacket pocket. 'Let's get the show on the road then. It's a great day to be on the river.'

Poor man, thought Albert, as Gordon and Nola disappeared with their guests. No love lost there. Wonder why he's bothered with them. Must be business, he assumed with remarkable acumen.

*　*　*

The club's marina was a simple jetty with berths for ten boats.

Gordon's boat, The Trident, a symphony in polished wood and gleaming brass, was first in line.

'That's her,' he announced proudly.

'It's beautiful,' said James with obvious sincerity. 'Really beautiful.'

Phyllis sniffed.

'We want everyone who goes on board to thoroughly enjoy themselves,' said Gordon, 'but we have just one rule; no shoes if you please. You'd be amazed at the amount of damage a simple pair of shoes, even with quite soft heels, can do to the woodwork.'

'No problem,' said James before Phyllis could get out a word of protest. 'You heard the man Phil ... shoes off.'

Phyllis decided not to make an issue of it. She had no doubt there would be other, meatier fights to pick.

Now barefoot, with their shoes stowed in a large canvas bag, the four climbed aboard. In the bows Nola cast off the mooring line, Gordon started the motor and the boat reversed away from the marina, its powerful motor rumbling below deck.

'We're not pushed for time today, are we?' Gordon inquired, edging the boat towards the centre of the river. 'There's so much to see once we get under way. It would be a shame to rush the day.'

'I agree,' said James. 'We're entirely at your disposal today, Gordon. We've got nothing on ... nothing to rush home for.'

'Gordon, dear,' said Phyllis playfully, 'I think you've forgotten something. The Andersons want us for drinks tonight. Don't tell you you'd forgotten already.'

'The Andersons?' Gordon asked, baffled. 'Who on earth are the Andersons.'

'The new people at number thirteen. I told you about it. All the neighbours will be there. We can't be the only ones in the street who don't turn up.'

'But I'm sure you never ....'

'Well, I'm sure I did. Anyway, we've got to be there at six or thereabouts.'

'It wouldn't matter if you're a few minutes late,' said Nola. 'No one's going to notice.'

Off to a brilliant start, thought Gordon, opening the throttle.

'It's got some power down there,' said James indicating the door leading below decks.

'I'll show you the engine later if you'd like. It's old but I've looked after it and it's just as powerful and reliable as anything they make today ... probably better in many ways. Now, who's for a beer?'

'A beer?' Phyllis inquired. 'I haven't drunk beer for years.'

'Then a G and T perhaps,' said Gordon, 'but it'll have to be from a can.'

'That'll do fine,' said James quickly.

Drinks were handed around and a toast to a great day

on the water was proposed and drunk without much enthusiasm.

'Look over there,' said Gordon pointing. 'See that white place on the waterfront. It's owned by that fellow who's just bought the power station in the Hunter valley.'

'You mean the fellow who's buying it so he can shut it down and make a few more billions out of renewable energy?' said James. It was more a statement than a question.

Gordon nodded. 'Yes. That's the fellow. Bloody crook if you ask me. Takes public money in subsidies to make more money for himself.'

'More fools us for electing a government that let's him get away with it,' said Nola.

'And the one just next to it,' said Gordon, pointing again, 'that's where the fellow lives who was on that dancing programme … or I should say lived there because I think he's in jail at the moment for assaulting someone or other in a bar. And the one behind it. I've never actually seen anyone there but the story is that it's owned by some Russian Oligarch that Putin's locked up because he was getting too big for his boots.'

As the day progressed it appeared that there were very few of the grand houses along the river front that did not have an interesting owner or history and Gordon was *au fait* with most of the details.

After about an hour's cruising Gordon turned out of the main channel into a small bay.

Nola hurried to the bow and dropped anchor.

'Might as well put in here and have our little picnic,' Gordon said, reaching under the bench for a large esky. 'We could go ashore and have it on the beach but we'd probably get a little damp with the tide as it is.'

Nola had been horrified at the amount of money Gordon spent on their 'little picnic.' 'They'll think we've got money to burn,' she had told him before they left home.

'And you know I don't eat crab,' she added angrily.

Gordon had nodded glumly. 'Yes, I know. But apparently *she* ... Phyllis ... loves it. James told me when we were discussing the arrangements.'

'I hope she chokes on it,' Nola said.

Phyllis love of crab was soon evident as the morsels quickly disappeared.

When the last of the food was eaten, scraps packed tidily in plastic bags and stowed, drinks handed around once more, Gordon started the motor and Nola returned to the bow to raise the anchor.

'Runs beautifully,' said James, listening to the subdued growl of the motor. 'Does it need much maintenance.'

Gordon, who had been looking for a credible segue to his purpose for the trip, seized the opening.

'No, luckily. I do all of the necessary maintenance so there are no big bills, which is just as well, because, well you know my financial position as well as anyone ... better in fact. I know your Dad mentioned to you that he'd told me about the shares ... what a sure thing they were.'

He continued with no attempt to keep the conversation

confidential. 'In fact, unless some sort of miracle happens for Nola and I we're going to have to sell the boat ... and probably the semi as well.'

When this dire prediction brought no reaction from James or Phyllis, Gordon continued. 'Of course I could try to borrow from somewhere but then I'd just be getting in deeper.'

He paused then gave a theatrical sigh. 'Of course we'd still be motoring along quite nicely if it wasn't for those shares. Of course I'd always trusted your Dad's judgment in the past, so naturally I thought I'd ...'

Phyllis cut him off. 'I heard that you actually went out and borrowed money to buy more of them.' she said bluntly. 'I can't tell you how many times I've heard James' father say never buy shares with borrowed money. Absolutely crazy thing to do ... that's what he said.'

'Yes, and of course he's right,' said Gordon. He shrugged, 'but it's done now and there's nothing I can do about it.' He turned to James. 'Nola and I would be immensely grateful if you could give us a hand out of our present pickle. I relied completely on your Dad when it came to money matters and he never once turned his back on me. I think we had a very good relationship, the two of us. He knew he could call on me for every little thing he needed doing around the house, and as you know it's a big old place with things always going wrong. And I did jobs at his other properties too ... he knew I'd go anywhere at a moment's notice to do whatever needed to be done. And I never asked much ...

just petrol if it was one of his places out of town. And as for material ... if I had to buy something to do a job I'd always bear the cost if it wasn't too expensive.'

James held up a hand. 'I know how highly Dad thought of you, Gordon, and I can tell you he did not take you for granted. He really appreciated everything you did for him. He often said how he couldn't do without you.

'But *he* lost a packet on those shares too. I suppose you know that. He'd been tied up with the company before they decided to go on the market and he put a great deal of his own money in. He was absolutely convinced their process would work and the shares would come on at a big premium. And I was in on it too ... big time. I promise you, Gordon, that there's a good deal of belt-tightening going on in our household right now. I've got an overdraft and I'm still paying off the mortgage on our place in the Mountains.'

'I thought you had a tenant in there,' said Nola. 'Wouldn't he be covering your mortgage.'

'Tenants come and go,' said Phyllis. 'And sometimes they don't pay their rent and skip out on you.'

'But you'd always have their bond. You wouldn't lose.'

'Is that what you think, is it Nola?' said Phyllis aggressively. 'It's easy to see you don't know anything about the pleasures of owning rental properties. We just had one lot of tenants skip out owing more than their bond was worth ... why the agent allowed them to get so far behind I've no idea and I'm going to report him. But that was the good news. When the bastards ran out they completely trashed the place. Shit everywhere ... I mean literally. Those are the sort of people you get landed with. They did it on purpose of course ... pure malice because we'd just put their rent up. It cost much more than the lousy bond to fix what they did before we could put a new lot in. It's not all beer and skittles in the rental market, Nola, I promise you.'

'Nice to own places to rent out,' said Nola with feeling. 'You don't have somewhere for us, do you ... somewhere nice and cheap. Or perhaps we'd be too much of a risk these days ... not enough money now to pay the bond let alone the rent.'

'I wouldn't know about that,' said Phyllis stiffly. 'We leave that sort of thing to the agents.'

James cringed. 'It's not as if we own rental properties all over the place. Gordon.'

Gordon nodded, eyes fixed on the water. 'As I recall your Dad owned quite a few, James. I visited most of them to do the odd job or two. I guess you'd own them all now ... since your brother Frank died.'

'Don't talk about that ... about Frank,' said Phyllis. 'You won't believe it but that bloody Valerie, Gordon's brother's widow, was onto our solicitor the same day the old man died. Thinks she's got some claim on the estate. She should live so long.' She turned to James. 'I hope that bloody solicitor of yours told her where to go. You'd better ring him and find out exactly what he told her. I don't trust him. Never have.'

James looked doubtful. 'He couldn't tell us what they talked about. That wouldn't be right. Client confidentiality you know.'

'Nonsense. He's our solicitor, not hers. But he wouldn't have to tell me anyway. It's obvious. She could smell the money and thought she could get her greedy hands on some of it. Well, good luck with that, Valerie. Besides, I'd be surprised if Brother Frank didn't leave her enough to keep going quite comfortably. I know he was an exceedingly boring man but he did have a decent job. What was he ... some sort of public servant, wasn't it? She'd have to have enough to go on with surely.'

Phyllis laughed unpleasantly.

Nola said softy. 'Unless she gambled.'

Three nuclear words.

Luckily the clubhouse was already in sight. Gordon swung the Trident in a shallow arc back towards the jetty. Nola went forward and jumped up nimbly onto the jetty's deck and made fast as the boat docked precisely.

'Time for a drink in the clubhouse?' Gordon asked. It was a formal invitation that demanded a refusal.

'No thanks, Gordon,' said James. 'Apparently we've got this function with the new neighbours. I'd forgotten all about that otherwise I'd be delighted.

'Another time perhaps,' he said, knowing there would never be another time.

* * *

Gordon stood on the verandah to wave as the Connaughts drove away. Nola was already at the bar, whisky in hand when Gordon joined her.

'Bastards, the pair of them,' she muttered said as he approached.

The barman, Albert, set down another whiskey. 'Not a happy day out?' he inquired.

Gordon shook his head as he reached for the drink. 'Understatement of the year, Albert.'

'Well, that's it, Gordon,' Nola said. 'We're on our own. There's no help there.'

'Oh I wouldn't say that,' said Gordon. 'I'll have another talk to him. And don't forget, as soon as things start going wrong at the big house he'll want help, because I don't think he's the sort of fellow who'd be happy getting in a plumber he doesn't know for $100 an hour plus call out charge. No. He'll be back to me like his Dad.'

'And you'd do it ... would you?' Nola looked up, eyes blazing. 'Make yourself on call twenty-four-seven for tips on the stock market.'

'If it means getting what we need to bail us out ... yes... anything.'

'Forget it, Gordon. It's not going to happen. Even if *he* wanted to help us that bitch would never let him do it.'

Gordon nodded. 'Yes, I'd have to agree she was pretty negative about helping.'

'Negative! That's putting it mildly. She'd never let it happen. And he wouldn't have the guts to stand up to her even if he wanted to help.'

'And you mentioning her little problem didn't help,' said Gordon. 'We weren't supposed to know about her gambling.

He told me about that in confidence. I should never have told you about it.'

'It wouldn't have made a scrap of difference. We were never going to get any money out of him so long as her fat arse points to the ground.'

Albert observed. 'Bit over-dressed, wasn't she, for a day on the water. Rather too showy for my taste.'

Nola nodded. 'Rather too showy for anyone's taste ... anyone with taste that is.'

They sipped their drinks.

Then Nola turned to James. 'I suppose you still have the keys to that house?'

Gordon frowned. 'Yes. Why.'

'Oh, nothing,' said Nola. She put her empty glass on the bar. 'Another two, Albert, if you please. And one for yourself.'

*   *   *

'Well, thank God that's over,' said Phyllis as James started the motor. 'I don't think I've ever spent such a more unpleasant couple of hours.'

James concentrated on his driving and offered no comment. He had a firm opinion about the source of any unpleasantness.

Phyllis continued. 'And you assured me as late as yesterday that they'd never even mention money. A wonderful judge of people you are. Hopeless. He could hardly wait to put the bite on you. And of course she was right there behind him all the way.'

'Of course she was,' said James. 'I don't think you realise just what a hole they're in, the pair of them.'

'Well it's a hole they dug for themselves, isn't it?'

'Yes, but with a lot of help from Dad. Don't forget that.'

'I haven't forgotten about your father's advice. But they were too quick to take it. And so were we. If he hadn't died *we'd* be going to him for a bail-out right now. But now we've got the estate to fall back on. Which reminds me; I want you to make sure that damned solicitor gets his finger out so we can get our hands on a bit of real money for a change, not the odd amounts your father graciously consented to dole out from time to time.'

James snapped angrily. 'That's not fair, Phyllis. Dad was very generous to us. Always.'

'He could have been a lot more generous. He certainly had the resources to make things much more comfortable for us. But Oh no ... we couldn't be treated like hot-house plants ... how many times did he tell us that. We had to learn to put down roots ... become established. What a lot of fanciful nonsense that was.'

'Well, that's the way he thought. He never had parents to dole out money whenever he ran short. He had to work hard to make it.'

'That's hardly an excuse for the way he treated us sometimes.'

It was an old argument and James knew better than to pursue it.

He asked. 'And why didn't you tell me about these new neighbours down the road and this so-called party?'

'Because there isn't one. I made it up because I knew you'd want an excuse to get away early.'

*   *   *

'And how'd it go ... your big day out on the water?'

William Berger and James Connaught were sitting on the same bench seat in the park opposite Frendz coffee shop.

James grimaced and shook his head. 'A disaster. A total disaster. I knew before we left home that it was a mistake to go. I should have rung the fellow up and said we were down with the virus or something ... anything.'

'And what was it all about ... the invitation? Did you find out. I thought he only knew your father ... not you.'

'And so he did. I'd never met the man before but Dad'd told me all about him. What a genius he was at fixing things ... at fixing everything ... plumbing, electrics, carpentry, gardening ... he even fixed a leak in the goldfish pond near Dad's front door.'

'You said you thought he was going to bite you for money. Did he?'

'Oh yes. That's what the whole thing was about. I knew that before we went. You see, when he did all the work around the house Dad'd take him out somewhere or other for a really good feed instead of giving him some cash in the hand. And as well as that he'd sometimes give him tips on the share market. Now Dad was really good with the share market. Tips from Dad were worth having. That's how he made his money. For years he'd been in with all the right people. He gave me tips from time to time and believe it or not they'd always come good. Some better than others of course, but sometimes that made a real difference for Phyl and I. If this handyman bloke, Gordon Tracey's his name, took Dad's advice over the years he was working around the house he'd have made good money too from Dad's tips ... very good money.

'Anyway the latest tip turned out to be a total disaster. It was on some company Dad'd been tied up with for ages. He'd worked up this special process for detoxifying land without having to cart it away and treat it off-site then bring it back. Great idea if it worked. Anyway, the day before the shares were due to come on the market there was this story in one of the papers that just blew it out of the water. And of course when the shares were listed they were way lower than we'd all paid for them. All the guys who days before were cursing their brokers for not getting them in on the float were thanking their lucky stars.

'But then it turned out that this Gordon fellah had not only put every cent he had into them but he'd even borrowed money to buy more. He's busted. He reckons he'll have to sell the boat now and maybe his house.'

William asked. 'And this Gordon reckoned it was up to you to bail him out?'

'Yes. Of course I explained that I'd lost money too and so had Dad ... all of which is true.'

'And how'd he take that?'

'He took it OK, but his wife, Nola ... a very tasty little piece ... she didn't take it at all well. And she and Phyl ... they didn't really hit it off at all. Then this Nola had to make some crack about Phyl's problem with the pokies. Of course that was the end of it. Luckily we were well on the way back to the boat club by then. I suppose I should never have said anything to Gordon about Phyl's problem but I never thought he'd tell his wife ... or anyone. And Nola and Phyl ... they'd been taking digs at each other from the moment we got there. Hate at first sight. When Nola dropped the gambling bomb Phyl was not amused.'

He smiled. 'You should have seen the gear Phyl thought was what the well-dressed lady sailor wore. You'd have thought she was going to a bloody ball or a Royal Garden Party or something; rings, bangles, pendants ... everything but her bloody tiara. I suppose that might have got up this Nola bird's nose seeing they'd just lost the lot.'

'Wouldn't be surprised,' said William.

'Anyway,' said James. 'Enough of that. Have you given any more thought to that idea of mine?'

'You mean I do your murder and you do mine?'

James nodded.

'Yes, I've thought about it but I still don't like it. It's too obvious really. The cops'd be onto us before you could say knife.'

James shook his head. 'Being onto us, as you put it, is one thing. Being able to prove something ... that's a different matter altogether.'

'Maybe, but I'm not some kind of criminal mastermind. I wouldn't have a clue how to go about actually killing someone … let alone getting away with it somehow. Besides, as I told you … I simply couldn't do it … kill someone … another human being. I abhor violence. Even at school I never got into fights or went in for any kind of physical sport where you might get hurt. No. I don't think I could do it.'

James was unwilling to accept a refusal. 'You say you don't *think* you couldn't do it. But you might. You never know. If having this Wisdom out of the way means you could get back your coffee shops … think about it again, William. Will you do that for me?'

William nodded. But it was not the sort of nod that gave James much hope.

*   *   *

'How much longer do you think they'll let us stay here?'

Nola was laying topless on the sun lounge tucked away in a corner of the tiny courtyard at the rear of their semi.

Gordon, leaning against the wall in a patch of sunlight, sipped coffee from a polystyrene mug. He shrugged. 'The bank you mean …. the mortgage. Depends, doesn't it … on what sort of story we an tell them.'

Nola looked up and tried to smile. 'You're not much of a one at telling stories, are you. Would you like me to have a word with them?'

'Try your feminine wiles you mean. Might have been worth a try once upon a time, but bank managers these days … zombies … robots … no discretion. Not like the old days when they could do favours for people they liked or thought deserved a break. Now rules are rules. No mates rates … stuff like that. No loyalty. Don't know the meaning of the word.'

He sighed and sipped his coffee.

Nola picked up a pair of sunglasses from the bricks beside her couch and put them on. 'The keys to the old man's house … you've still got them.' It wasn't a question.

'Yes, I told you. Why do you ask? James never asked for them back.'

'Perhaps he doesn't know you've got them.'

Gordon shook his head. 'Hardly likely. He knew I used to go over to the house and check things … do things like painting while the old man was away overseas. He liked any painting done then so he wouldn't be bothered by the smell. James must have known I had keys to get into the place … to come and go.'

'And he hasn't mentioned them …asked about them?'

'No. I told you. If he had I'd have given them back.'

'Well it's a damned good thing you didn't.'

'Oh, and why's that?' Gordon asked uneasily.

'Because I'm going over there one night soon … very soon … and I'm going to take every piece of jewellery that bitch owns.'

Gordon was shocked. 'Nola! You can't do that. I know how you feel about her, but you can't just …'

'It's not a matter of how I feel about her. It's how I feel about everything that's been going on. About you working for that tight old bastard anytime he wanted some little thing done that he could have got any tradesman to do ... and then paying you off with tips on the share market and the odd meal out somewhere.'

Gordon waved an arm. 'Look it was fine with me. I enjoyed doing it. I was semi-retired anyway, remember. I was glad of a few things to do around the place ... to keep me occupied. There was plenty to do there. And you weren't always sorry to have me out of the house as I recall. But actually breaking in and stealing ...'

Nola scrambled off the sun lounge and replaced her top. 'Hold it there for one moment, Gordon. Let's get a few facts straight here. For a start there'd be no question of us breaking in. You have a key, right. We wouldn't be breaking in. And as for stealing. We'd only be taking what's our by right.'

Gordon shook his head. 'You might be technically right about not breaking in. But stealing. We'd have a pretty tough time convincing a judge and jury that because her father-in-law hadn't paid me in cash at the award rate that gave us the right to take that woman's jewellery.'

'I'm talking about moral rights,' said Nola. 'Things people like them know nothing about. You saw all that stuff she wore on the boat. How much d'you think it was worth? Go on. Guess.'

'I've no idea. And how do you know it was all real ... not bling.'

Nola curled a lip. 'Oh come on Gordon. Why do you think she was wearing it. Do you think she'd've had it on if it was costume jewellery. She was there to show off ... to rub our noses in it. That stuff was worth more than the boat five times over.'

'Well, you'd know so I won't argue about it.'

'And another thing; didn't the old man once tell you something about Gordon having a girl friend ... a girl he used to visit every week, regular as clock work.'

Gordon nodded, smiling. 'Yes, I'd forgotten all about that. There's nothing wrong with your memory. The old man was very amused about it. Thought it was a wonderful joke ... poor submissive down-trodden little James sneaking out every Wednesday night to get his end in, and Phyllis not having a clue about it. She thought he was out playing chess somewhere. But that was a while ago. It mightn't still be going on, particularly now that he's come into money. He might make a few changes in his lifestyle. Get a new more upmarket mistress, who knows.'

'Maybe you're right,' said Nola thoughtfully. 'But I'd say tonight's as good a time as any to find out if he's still up to his old tricks. Are you coming?'

Gordon smiled. 'Well, we don't have any other engagements so far as I'm aware. Not even a neighbourhood party down the road. So why not? Our own little surveillance operation. We can an pretend we're private detectives on a stake out. Beats TV any time.

'Now, what does the well-dressed burglar wear these days?'

Kenny Abbott and Fricka Glassop had just disengaged after a vigourous bout of love-making in the back of Kenny's distinctively decorated station wagon.

Kenny pushed up the tailgate, climbed down and headed for a pee in the privacy of the surrounding dark bushland of the national park.

Fricka had just pulled on her jeans when Kenny returned. Even in the dim light thrown by the single bulb in the back of the wagon Fricka could see Kenny was excited.

'Hey, Fricka. Guess what I just found in the bushes over there? A body. Some old sheila.'

'A body,' Fricka repeated anxiously. 'Are you sure she's dead?'

'Course she's dead. She's been all beat up. There's blood all over her.'

Fricka was not inclined to doubt Kenny's expertise in matters relating to sudden death and murder because these were the stock-in-trade of his family.

Kenny's Uncle Raymond was the most senior member of a local crime gang that specialised in drug distribution, and in pursuit of their trade the family were no strangers to violence and sudden death.

'So what are you going to do about her?' Fricka asked. 'If she's really dead I reckon you should just leave her there for some else to find. You don't want to get mixed up with it, Kenny, do you? I mean there'd have to be the police called in and everything.'

Kenny nodded. 'Yeah. You're right. We don't want that. So wadda you reckon, Fricka?'

Fricka shrugged. 'Why ask me? Why not ring your Uncle Ray and ask him? He'd know wouldn't he … what to do when you find a body?'

Kenny brightened. 'Yeah. Good idea. Uncle Ray. He'd know what to do with her.'

He took the mobile phone from his back pocket and stabbed a finger at the keypad. 'Uncle Ray,' he said, 'It's Kenny here. Hey, guess what I just found?'

From where she sat Fricka could hear Uncle Ray telling his nephew in plain, fruity language that it was too late at night to be playing idiotic guessing games.

'I found a body … Fricka an' me. Some old sheila looked like she'd been in a fight.'

There followed a conversation punctuated by Uncle Ray interposing questions or offering comments.

As the conversation progressed it became plain to Fricka that Uncle Ray did not share Kenny's enthusiasm at the discovery.

At last Kenny ended the call with the thrust of a thumb.

'Uncle Ray said to get rid of her,' he announced glumly.

'Get rid of her?' Fricka echoed. 'But someone's already done that, haven't they … got rid of her … or so you reckon.'

'Yeah, but he didn't mean *that* sort of get rid of her. He said we couldn't leave her there now. We've got to move her somewhere else.'

'Why?' Fricka asked sensibly. 'Why move her? She's all right there, isn't she? I mean she doesn't care where she is.'

'No, of course she doesn't. I know that. But we've got to move her on account of the cops. Uncle Ray said if we leave her there and she's found the cops are going to get onto us straight away. Someone'll dob on us for sure and they'll blame us for what ever happened to her. They always blame us ... for everything.'

'But the cops'd never know we were here. How'd they find out?'

'Uncle Ray said there's always lots of couples hang out around here and we could have been seen ... and my wagon stands out a mile. Besides, he said there'd be our tyre tracks and things like that. The cops'd be right onto us.'

Fricka was not about to argue the toss with Kenny's Uncle Ray, although she did not share his concern about the police using their tyre marks as a means of identifying them since she had noticed a jumble of different tyre tracks on the muddy dirt road into the area which was a busy Lovers' Lane.

She asked. 'Did he say where to put her?'

Kenny shook his head. 'No, but I guess it'd have to be a fair way away. Somewhere the cops won't find our tyre tracks.'

Fricka frowned. 'But if we drive her somewhere else we're going to leave tyre tracks getting there, aren't we, unless we carry her somewhere else, and I'm not up for that.'

'OK,' said Kenny with an air of resignation. 'Well, let's

get her in the back first then we can decide what to do about her.'

It was not the way Fricka had expected the evening to end … carrying a bloodied and badly disfigured woman's body from where she lay under a pile of leaves and twigs, fifty yards to the back of her boyfriend's van. The things one did for love, she thought.

'You take her head and I'll take her feet. OK?' Kenny suggested.

'But the head's the heavy end,' sad Fricka. 'I might drop her.'

'Bloody rubbish,' said Benny. 'She's not that heavy and you don't have to carry her far … just to the van.'

Fricka shook her head. She didn't like any of this, but then if you went out with Benny you had to expect strange things to happen sometimes.

When they were in position Benny said: 'Now, one, two, three …. lift.'

The woman was as heavy as Fricka had expected and she struggled to keep hold of her burden.

At last when they were settled in the van Benny said. 'I don't see why we should have to take her far. Besides, I'm getting bloody low on petrol.

Fricka suggested. 'What about we take her to that other spot just up the road. You know. Where we went for your birthday.'

Benny brightened. 'Yeah, Good idea, Fricka. That's only a coupla hundred yards if that. It's not far down off the road.

I'll head for there.'

Benny started the motor, reversed, turned and headed back up the rough track to join Kanundda Head Road.

He turned left and drove slowly with lights on high beam. 'It's just along here somewhere, right?'

'Yeah, not far,' said Fricka. 'I'll keep an eye out. You watch the road.'

They had been traveling for less than a minute when Fricka said: 'There it is, just up ahead. Slow down ... now turn here.'

Benny turned the wagon carefully off the road, scanning the bush ahead for some entry. Then he saw two narrow rutted tracks with vegetation growing between them that led down into the dark bush.

'Are you sure this is the way?' he asked.

'I'm not sure of anything,' said Fricka. 'But even if it's not the same place let's see go on and see what's down there anyway. This's got to lead somewhere and it's probably going to be a good as anywhere.'

They had gone only a short distance before the wagon pushed through a group of low shrubs into a small clearing. 'Yeah I remember this spot,' said Benny. 'This'll do fine. Now come'n we'll get her out.'

They climbed out and Benny raised the tailgate. 'Right. Now I'll take her feet and you take her by the shoulders. Right?'

'But that's the heavy end,' Fricka protested again, she added. 'And she's heavier than she looks. I nearly dropped her back there.'

43

'Aw stop goin' on. We'll take her just a little way then dump her. OK?'

'OK. Just a little way.'

'Now, One, two, three … lift.'

The ungainly procession had covered less than twenty paces before Fricka lost her grip.

The lady, disheveled and bloody, fell from Fricka's hands. Her head landed heavily on a small outcrop of granite uncovered by recent heavy rain.

'Be careful,' said Benny, seeing Fricka's distress. 'Now just get hold of her again. Here I'll take her head this time if you reckon she's too heavy for you. Then we'll put her down just over here and we'll cover here up with a few leaves and things.'

Near tears Fricka said. 'Promise you'll ring in and tell the coppers where she is, because if you don't I will.'

'I'll ring in, don't worry,; Benny snapped. 'I don't know why you're in such a state about her. I mean she's not worrying about it, is she?'

What Benny didn't know was the reason Fricka had dropped her burden.

She had decided to say nothing about it, but Fricka was quite certain she had seen the woman's eyes flicker moments before she lost her grip.

She had considered mentioning this phenomenon to Benny but feared that he may decide to take further advice from Uncle Ray and God alone knew what complications that may led to.

So best to say nothing, but make sure that the relevant authorities knew where the lady was to be found ... and soon.

*　　*　　*

Among the tyre tracks that Fricka had noticed as Benny first drove down into the bush was a very distinctive set left by an imported sports car driven by Corey Wisdom.

These tracks were distinctive not only from the design of the imprints left behind by the imported tyres, but by their extraordinary width.

But Corey was oblivious to such details as he sat in the car adjusting his clothes while the woman beside him, Angela Bly, who worked as supervisor over his chain of coffee shops, did the same.

When he bought the car he had not thought it would be used so frequently to accommodate this particular activity and he had discovered that it was not at all unusual for his partners to complain about the inconvenience of making love in a vehicle so obviously not fit for purpose.

He had even encountered refusals at the crucial moment.

But his present company had not protested when it came to the point although she had become uncomfortable when caught in the headlights of vehicles descending the steep track to the area and others departing. It had turned out to be a rather busy spot.

It was one of these cars, or rather its occupant, a woman,

that particularly caught Corey's attention. Corey had watched with more than passing interest when the woman got out of the car and stood briefly in the headlights talking to a man who had arrived at the same time in another vehicle.

It seemed to Corey that this couple had much more serious business in mind than he. Their conversation was becoming quite agitated. The woman ... he thought he recognised her but could not put a name to the face ... was shaking an angry finger at the man.

Corey frowned. Now, where had he seen her before. If he didn't try too hard it might come to him. Perhaps she was a regular at one of his coffee shops. Perhaps that was where he had seen her. In fact, now that he thought of it he felt certain that it was at his coffee shop in the St James Shopping Village that he had seen her, and more than once. Yes. If she was a regular there she certainly would be remembered, by the male staff anyway. He would make inquiries there and meanwhile he would try to get a sneaky photo of her for identification purposes.

As he watched the two broke off their argument and both went to the woman's car and climbed in. The motor started and then, surprisingly, the car turned and very slowly edged deeper into the bush along a little-used narrow track.

Corey knew from experience that this track ended in a cul-de-sac after about fifty metres and the driver then had to reverse out as there was no space to turn a car.

But what on earth could they be doing down there. They

were not lovers, that was certain from the body language he had witnessed. But they were up to something, that was obvious, and Corey wanted to know what that something was.

He reached up, switched the car's internal light to off and opened the door.

'Where are you going,' Angela asked.

'Wait here, love,' he said. 'I won't be a moment.'

In fact nearly ten minutes passed before Corey returned.

'Well?' Angela asked.

'Well what?' said Corey. He had no intention of sharing with anyone the interesting things he had just seen.

'What was that about?' the supervisor persisted. 'Who were those people you were so interested in? And what on earth were they up to down there?'

But Corey just shook his head. 'Time to go home,' he said.

But before he started the car he took out his phone. From where she sat Angela could see the screen. Corey had written what appeared to be two numberplates in his phone.

'That the girl's car, is it? Angela asked. 'Fancy her, do you?'

Corey smiled. 'Not the way you think.' He didn't bother to mention that he had taken a photo of the woman by the light of a powerful lantern the couple had used to illuminate their extraordinary task.

Then he said. 'I'm going to send you two number plates. I want you to find the owners for me first thing in the morning. OK?'

*   *   *

William Berger had just put down his book and turned off the bedside light when he heard the landline downstairs ring.

Who on earth can that be ringing at this hour? Damn them, he thought. If it's important they'll leave a message or ring back in the morning.

Sure enough there was a message waiting when William picked up the phone after preparing his usual breakfast of coffee and toast.

He was surprised to see the message was from James Connaught.

'Wonder what he's on about now. I suppose he wants an answer about his murder idea. Well no thanks, James. I've no wish to spend my declining years in some miserable jail, thank you very much.'

He put down his coffee and played the message.

James voice came through the tiny speaker as a harsh whisper.

'Congratulations, William. I'd almost given up on you. It seems you had a lot more guts than you gave yourself credit for. Not the sort of result I'd expect from someone who reckoned they couldn't stand the sight of blood. There was blood everywhere. It was enough to turn *my* stomach, I can tell you and I'm not particularly squeamish.

'And from the look of things I'd say she must have put up quite a fight. I'd've loved to have been a fly on the wall. Now, a word of advice if I may … if she bruised you or cut you … and I'd say she must have done some damage by the look of her bedroom … you'll have to have some explanation ready for that … how you got your injuries. And there could be some of your skin under her fingernails if she got her claws into you. The police will be straight onto that … the assailants skin under the victim's fingernails, first thing they look for. That's why the first thing they do in cases like this is put bags over the hands of murder victims. So if you've still got her body somewhere handy you should have a look at things like that and clean under her nails.

'Oh and I assume you wore gloves. That would have been pretty elementary.

'And I assume you somehow got in without a key but without leaving any signs of a break-in. The cops seem to be pretty sure of that. They think either she knew the person and let him in or that it's an inside job — meaning me — so it's a damn good thing I've got good alibi.

'And of course we shouldn't be talking like this on the phone, so delete this message as soon as you've played it.'

William listened to this stream of advice open-mouthed, stunned.

The scratchy voice continued. 'But I'd love to know where you put her … the body. And don't worry about the jewellery. I assume you took it. You're welcome to it. She had it well insured. Of course I'll have to ring the police if I'm going to make a claim and I expect I'll have to make a missing persons report in a day or two unless you left her somewhere she's going to be found soon. It might become a problem for me if you've hidden her too well and I have to wait the seven years to have her declared dead. Not that I'd want to get married again in a hurry, that's for sure, but you never know what other sort of legal complications might arise in the future. Give me a ring as soon as you like and perhaps we should arrange to meet to work out where we go from here. Don't forget to delete this tape. Do it now. If the cops find it we're done.'

William shook his head in bewilderment.

There could be no doubt what had happened. Phyllis Connaught had disappeared in circumstances that had convinced her husband that she had been murdered during the course of a burglary.

And the most important aspect of the call was that James was convinced that he, William Burger, was responsible, which in the light of their recent conversations was a reasonable assumption.

But what to do about it?

James had suggested a meeting, but that was out of the question. William knew in a face to face meeting he could never maintain the deception that he had actually done it.

What were his option?

First he could accept James assumption that he had murdered Phyllis Connaught and made away with her body. He could refuse to say how he had done it and where he had hidden her body, offering the sensible explanation that the fewer who knew about it the better.

So now James Connaught would feel himself under an obligation to do *his* murder …. kill Corey Bloody Wisdom.

Yes, he liked that idea …. he liked it very much.

But he had doubts about his ability to see the charade through. He did not have the acting or improvisational skills to come up with convincing answers to questions that James would certainly throw at him. How did he get into the house? There was no sign of a break in so did he somehow pick a lock … a rather esoteric skill, William thought, and one which James was not likely to think he had acquired.

Then there was the question of the jewellery. What did he intend to do with the jewellery which of course he did not have. The thief couldn't just take it to a pawn broker and sell it because everyone knew that police advised all those in the trade to be on the look out for stolen jewellery.

After giving the matter further thought he decided that his best course, when he rang James, was simply to say nothing … to refuse to discuss the matter in any detail for the sensible reason that the fewer people who knew about the matter the safer they both would be.

If at some stage James got difficult about the jewellery and wanted it returned he could say he had to take it to make it look like a burglary gone wrong and that he'd sold it cheaply somewhere to a stranger in a pub just to be rid of it. How often did one read about that sort of thing in the press. The burglar breaks in; the lady of the house wakes up, defends her jewellery and gets killed in the process. Anyway, he could tell James that the jewellery should be treated as spoils of war and as such he was entitled to keep it. Which would have been nice if he actually had the things.

Yes, he would leave it a while, ring James, tell him nothing, or as little as possible, make it clear that he expect James to keep his end of the bargain and hang up.

*   *   *

In his downstairs study James put the receiver down thoughtfully. What a strange conversation it had been. William had seemed almost surprised when he had described the chaos he had discovered in his bedroom when he arrived home.

That detective who came in response to his call, what was his name, Burke, Donald Burke, had jumped to all the right conclusions. The burglar had come in through the bathroom window (William had the foresight to open the catch before the police arrived) so there was no question of it being an inside job and suspicion falling on him.

Then when he had told the detective that Phyl's jewellery was missing the question of motive was accounted for. And then there was all that blood. One of those scientific fellows had found under their bed a piece of tissue paper with a blood-stained foot print on it ... a heel-print to be precise the scientific fellow thought.

He had taken it away for analysis.

Detective Burke had commented that footprints weren't as good as fingerprints when it came to evidence in court, but they were a good place to start although there was no big police record system for footprints like there was for fingerprints, so they'd be very unlikely to find a match.

Well, Alleluia to that, thought James. Still, there was a long way to go and they'd both have to hold their nerves.

It was a bit of a worry that the copper had taken away Phyl's diary. He didn't know she even kept a bloody diary. God knows what nonsense the stupid woman wrote in it. All fantasy, most likely.

At least the cops didn't know of any connections between William and he. And best to keep it that way.

*   *   *

Edgar Hodgkiss was sitting on one of the curved benches surrounding the well-kept redwood table on the back deck of the bungalow in suburban Lillimoor which he shared with his daughter, Esme, and her husband, Detective Inspector Donald Burke.

Hodgkiss had just solved the chess problem which he had clipped neatly from the weekend papers and which now lay discarded on the table. It had not posed a great challenge; a waiting move with the white king, black made a forced move with a bishop which left the black king prey to an obvious checkmate.

Now Hodgkiss was waiting in the hope that his son-in-law would come home for lunch, as he sometimes did when investigation some crime committed nearby.

Hodgkiss had woken during the night to see the light on in the Burke's bedroom which was opposite his own room at the front of the house.

He had heard a whispered conversation in the hallway outside his door then soon he had heard Donald's unmarked police car, parked in the driveway, start up. Moments later the headlights of the departing vehicle had swept across his bedroom ceiling as Donald turned the car in the street and drove away.

Hodgkiss knew that it was not at all unusual for Donald to be called out in the middle of the night to attend some crime scene and experience had shown that late night call-outs usually were to a serious crime.

Perhaps it's a murder, Hodgkiss had thought with unconscious relish, because Hodgkiss had more than a passing interest in crime ... particularly in those crimes which his son-in-law was called on to investigate.

It was now nearly ten years since Hodgkiss had arrived unannounced on the Burke's doorstep with all his worldly possessions crammed into two ancient leather suitcases.

Following the death of his wife of forty years, Hodgkiss had sold the family home ... he had pronounced it 'surplus to my needs' ... and moved into a nearby boarding house which he shared with the owner, a middle-aged widow with few cooking skills, and two other lodgers.

Hodgkiss, a retired schoolteacher, did not suffer fools lightly and soon mealtimes at the boarding house became prolonged debating sessions as Hodgkiss rarely found common ground with the others on any topic.

The debates often became quite heated and it was not long before Hodgkiss was asked to pack his bags and move on.

Over the following months Hodgkiss percolated through a series of increasingly seedy boarding houses until at last he decided that life with his daughter was his only rational option.

Esme, who had been following her father's moves from one place to the next with growing alarm, was secretly relieved when he arrived. She had followed his rapid deterioration from an alert senior, who daily did three crossword puzzles and read newspapers from front to back, to nothing more than a couch potato, often to be found slumped in front of some vacuuous television programme in the guests' lounge of his current boarding house, usually asleep or with the sound turned off.

So when he arrived she was secretly relieved, glad to have him on hand where she could supervise him in her caring but no-nonsense manner.

But Donald was not at all in favour. He agreed grudgingly to allow Hodgkiss to stay on the strict proviso that he remain only for as long as it took him to find other accommodation.

This condition however was soon relaxed then abandoned when Hodgkiss demonstrated a remarkable talent for solving crime.

It first showed itself one evening when Donald, then

a detective sergeant, and his superior officer, Inspector O'Hare, were sitting at the redwood setting on the back deck discussing the details of a particularly baffling case they were currently investigating.

They were unaware of Hodgkiss presence at the other end of the deck where he sat in a director's chair, apparently engrossed in a chess magazine.

At one point Hodgkiss lowered the magazine, cleared his throat to get their attention, then suggested a new line of inquiry. Recognising its possibilities Inspector O'Hare took up the suggestion which involved simply asking one of the witnesses some unlikely questions which had previously gone unasked. The surprising answers led to the immediate arrest and quick conviction of a person not previously a suspect.

That was the first of many occasions when suggestions from Hodgkiss resulted in Donald finding sometimes spectacular solutions to his cases.

Consequently his career had flourished. He rose rapidly to the rank of Detective Inspector with a reputation for solving the most complex and tricky criminal puzzles, often as the result of surprising and original insights.

No one outside the Burke household, with the exception of Mr O'Hare, now a Superintendent, knew the source of these inspired leaps, and Hodgkiss was not bothered to have any credit put his way. Donald's progress through the ranks meant more money for the family and that was enough for him.

Any observer of this arrangement, had there been one,

might have concluded that Hodgkiss and Donald, as allies in fighting crime, were naturally friends and allies in all matters.

Nothing would have been further from the truth.

The problem was that Hodgkiss could neither understand nor excuse Donald's failure to make the same observations and reach the same conclusions as himself.

That, combined with his intolerance, the same negative quality that had made his living in boarding houses untenable, was very soon on display in the Burke household.

For example, after offering a solution to one of Donald's investigations he could not resist adding: 'Really Donald, I would have thought that anyone with even a modicum of intelligence we have seen that.'

This was typical of the pointed barbs which Hodgkiss invariably delivered when offering some advice or solutions.

Now the word 'obvious' was banned in the Burke household since Hodgkiss used it so often in derogatory comments on Donald's investigative skills.

Thus Esme was often hard pressed to keep the peace between her husband and her father.

Just then Hodgkiss heard a car pull into the driveway. The motor stopped. A door slammed and there came the sound of heavy feet on the gravel drive.

Then Donald appeared at the foot of the short wooden steps leading up to the deck.

He nodded. 'Yeah. I thought I might find you here. Laying in wait.'

'Nothing of the sort,' said Hodgkiss. 'I was just doing the

chess problem. Now. What's happened. Last night I heard you ...'

Donald held up a large blunt-fingered hand. 'Hold your horses just a minute, Dad. I know what you want. Just give a fellah a chance to get a bite of lunch inside him first. OK?'

Just then Esme pushed aside the heavy sliding door from the family room and stepped out on the deck, a large platter of cheese and tomato sandwiches in one hand and two mugs of black tea gripped perilously in the other.

'I thought you both might like to have your lunch out here' she said setting down the plate and mugs. 'It's a nice morning.'

'Thank you, Esme,' said Hodgkiss. 'Very thoughtful of you. And it saves time.'

'Saves time?' Esme asked, puzzled.

Donald explained with a nod in Hodgkiss' direction. 'He means he doesn't have to wait while I eat my lunch before he hears about .... you know ... what happened up the road.'

Esme nodded. 'All right. But don't you bolt it down, Donald. It won't do that ulcer any good if you don't chew your food properly.'

'Up the road, was it?' Hodgkiss asked. 'Not far away then.'

'Edmund Street. Woman abducted ... or so it seems.'

'Or so it seems?' Hodgkiss echoed. 'You think it's not that simple then?'

'Early days,' said Donald, taking a large bite from a sandwich.

'Then you've got doubts then, have you … about what happened? Anything obviously wrong.'

Donald shrugged and swallowed a large mouthful with difficulty. 'Not obviously. The missing woman is one Phyllis Connaught. Her husband, James, was out at the time. He's one of your mob … chess mad. He was out at his chess club when it happened. He goes there every Wednesday night without fail. Or so he says. Of course we'll have to check his story.'

'And what happened? Did they break in, whoever did it?'

Donald shook his head. 'Bathroom window left open. Must have got in that way, although there's no sign that anyone actually did, because there's a garden bed under the window and there's no dirt on the sill or anywhere inside as you might expect.'

Hodgkiss nodded. 'So it was probably an inside job.'

'I certainly haven't rule it out,'

'Anything missing … apart from Mrs Connaught?'

'Yeah. Jewellery. A lot of it. Valuable stuff too, according to the husband. He'd already made out a list of the things for the insurance company. There're photos of some of it. A photo of the wife wearing a ring and a necklace. Of course they were all taken in the distance so they mightn't be much help with insurance. But there were photos of her with bracelets on and they were more close up. Really fond of her jewellery, that lady.'

'Then she wouldn't have gone quietly,' Hodgkiss observed.

'She certainly did not. Put up quite a fight. Blood

everywhere. Looks like whoever did it took her down the internal stairs to the basement then away, probably in her own car because according to her husband it's missing.'

'Enough blood to suggest that she might not have had enough left to survive?'

Donald shook his head. 'Oh no. She'd have had enough left to keep ticking over. And another thing; the scene of crime boys found a bloody footprint ... or rather a heel print ... on a scrap of tissue under the bed.'

Hodgkiss eyebrows rose. 'Oh? Well that could certainly come in handy if your ever find a heel to compare it with.'

'Yeah, maybe, but it's not quite as handy as a bloodstained fingerprint. Judges and juries aren't all that happy about footprints. Not the same positive feel about them.

'And even if we had a perfect match it wouldn't be a lay down misere that it's the guy we want. There's been quite a lot of work done on the subject. In fact when I mentioned it in the office it turns out that Sanderson knew all about it ... as you'd expect.'

Sergeant Sanderson was Donald's regular partner in investigations and was the butt of jokes and often severe criticism for his pedantic approach to some aspects of police work. Donald was often frustrated by the length of time Sanderson took to take down witnesses' statements ... insisting upon every word being recorded.

'Sanderson said he'd read that there's less than a one in a billion chance that there could be two identical footprints in the world, but there's some questions about the methods used in that research so footprints aren't a silver bullet.'

Hodgkiss shrugged. 'Pity. Anything else of interest at the crime scene? Anything I can help with?' he asked nonchalantly.

Donald shook his head then paused and pushed back from the table. 'Yeah. Come to think of it, there *is* something you could have a look at for me. It seems the missing lady kept a diary. I asked the husband would he mind if I took it away to have a look-see if there was anything there to help us, and he said OK. Apparently he had no idea she kept a diary. It's in the car. Hang on. I'll get it for you.'

Donald rose and headed for the driveway Moments later he was back with a black-covered pocket-sized diary. He dropped it on the table in front of Hodgkiss. 'There you are, Dad. Not a lot in it. I've had a quick look through. Nothing about kidnappers threatening to come and get her. Just appointments. Stuff like that. Have a look and let me know if there's anything takes your fancy as a decent clue.'

Hodgkiss smiled. Good. He had something constructive to do.

He picked up the book and opened it.

*   *   *

If Hodgkiss expected the diary to prove a gold mine of revealing insights he was soon disappointed.

Entries were few and mostly conveyed nothing of interest.

In January there were three entries ... each on a Monday

61

in the a.m. section of the page. 'Meeting JK.'

Hodgkiss shook his head in disappointment as he skipped through the small book.

There was only one entry that caught his attention for more than a moment. It was on the Sunday of the previous weekend. It read: **BBCC Trident N and G noon Wednesday.**

Hodgkiss paused. That would have been last Wednesday. Now, he thought, Trident. What does the name Trident suggest. Some association with the sea. Something maritime ... marine ... King Neptune. Yes, that could be safely assumed. A boat, perhaps.

Now for the BBCC part.

Well, the terminal C would likely be a club of some kind. But CC ... a cricket club, perhaps.

But how did that relate to the sea or a boat.

Hodgkiss took the phone from his shirt pocket an began search of local clubs starting with BB.

After a very short search the name Buccaneers' Bay Cruising Club appeared on his screen.

Hodgkiss smiled. It was the only BBCC in the vicinity, in fact the only BBCC club in the State. Yes, a visit to the Buccaneers' Bay Cruising Club would be as good a place as any to begin his investigation, because Hodgkiss had already decided that this was a matter in which he would take a personal interest.

In recent weeks Donald had been assigned to desk duties consequently Hodgkiss had been deprived of the opportunity to assist in an investigation and the boredom had been weighing heavily on him.

If Donald inquired whether any of the diary entries had proved of interest Hodgkiss had decided that he would simply shake his head. After all, it was highly unlikely this rather out-of-the-way boat club that he had never heard of would turn out to have any connection with this rather dramatic crime.

So, after dinner, when Hodgkiss and Donald were sitting in the family room waiting for Donald's favourite quiz programme to begin, Donald announced: 'Well, we found that woman's car ... Mrs Connaught's.'

'Oh. Did you? Where?' Hodgkiss asked, trying not to sound at all interested.

'Just off Kanundda Head Road. In one of those Lovers' Lane spots.'

'And she wasn't in it, I assume.'

'No. But she left a fair bit of her blood behind. I suppose it was hers.'

'And what made you look there.'

'Someone rang in ... a man ... in the middle of the night. The local boys only got around to having a look just now.'

'I don't suppose he left a name ... the man who rang in.'

'No way. Probably wouldn't want anyone to know he was there. People go there for only one reason usually.'

'No sign of the woman then? Hodgkiss asked.

'No. But she'll turn up soon.'

The quiz was about to start when the phone in Donald's jacket pocket sounded his ringtone, *John Peel.*

As Donald listened to the call Hodgkiss saw a look of irritation appear on his son-in-law's face.

'Bad news?' he asked when the call ended.

'They've found her ... that woman ... Mrs Connaught. Dead. Not far from the spot we were told about first.'

Hodgkiss nodded. 'So it's murder then.'

'Yeah. Looks that way. That was Sanderson on the blower. He reckons they've found where she was dumped the first time. Forensics found tyre tracks everywhere. Now they're going to try to locate some of the owners and see if they noticed anything.'

'Do we know who found her ... the second time?'

Donald shook his head. 'Nah. Not yet. Man's voice again according to the officer who took the call. Sounded like a young guy he thought. No name though,' he said pushing up from the lounge. 'I'll have to be getting out there.'

'I don't suppose you'd like some company, would you, Donald?' Hodgkiss asked without much hope.

Donald turned at the door. 'No thanks dad. I think this will turn out to be a pretty straight forward case.'

'Not an abduction then ... like the husband thought.'

'No way.' said Donald confidently. 'Real panic-merchant, that fellah. We'll soon find out what happened to her,' he said, then added, 'and Mr Connaught might have a question or two to answer when we do. It's usually the husband, right Dad?'

'Yes, Donald,' said Hodgkiss. 'But not always,' he cautioned. But Donald was gone.

Minutes later, after he had heard the car leave, Hodgkiss hurried through to the kitchen where Esme was unpacking the dishwasher.

'Do you have any plans for tomorrow?' he asked innocently.

Esme looked up sharply. 'No. Why do you ask?'

'Have you ever heard of a place called Buccaneer's Bay?'

Esme shook her head, puzzled. 'No. Why?'

'Because I need to go there ... very soon ... to the Buccaneer's Bay Cruising Club ... and there's no need for Donald to know.'

* * *

Next morning, with the assistance of a contact at the Kanundda Council ... an officer responsible for levying fines on motorists who overstayed their welcome in council car parks ... Angela Bly soon discovered who owned the two vehicles that had piqued the interest of her boss, Corey Wisdom, during their bushland tryst.

One of the vehicles belonged to a Gordon Tracey, presumably the man they had seen arguing with the woman last night, and the other belonged to a Phyllis Connaught.

Neither name meant anything to either Angela or later to Wisdom when she passed on the information.

But Corey did not seem disappointed with these results and later that morning he headed for his coffee shop in the St James Shopping Village, a popular venue for the upwardly-mobile young matrons of the surrounding area.

After a single glance at the screen of Corey's phone the shop manager, an ambitious young man with severe acne, gave a name to the image. 'That's Nola Tracey. I'd know her anywhere. She's a regular. Not easy to forget, that one. Lives in Hyperion Street … number 18. She's got an account with us. Good customer. Husband comes with her sometimes.' This rider he added as a caution, being aware of his employers preferences.

So now Corey had added a name and an address to his photo. Nothing more was needed. Time to take steps. No point in delaying. He hurried back to his office.

When Angela came in later in the day with her weekly report on the chain's progress towards meeting the various monetary targets Corey had set, she found him examining the image of a row of semis on his computer screen.

'Thinking of moving?' she asked. 'No. That would be seriously down-sizing if you were thinking of moving there.' Another thought crossed her mind. 'More likely you've been doing a bit of detective work of your own because that's where she lives, right … the rather attractive, argumentative lady from last night? Well, it certainly didn't take you long to track her down, did it? You must be really keen. What now?'

Corey smiled but said nothing. It was the 'what now" that was exercising his mind.

Why wait? Corey reached for his phone, pulled down a menu and stabbed a finger at the keypad.

In the rather chic semi in Hyperion Street, Nola Tracey was surprised when the landline phone rang.

Now who on earth could that be. None of our friends ring us on that number these days. Probably one of those nuisance calls. I'll have to have the damned thing disconnected. Should have done it long ago.

She lifted the handset. 'Yes. who is it?' she asked.

*　　*　　*

Finding the Buccaneer's Bay Cruising Club presented no problems. Esme followed the instructions from the satellite guidance system in her phone and an hour after leaving home Esme was stopping her small beige sedan in the club's car park.

Nevertheless the trip had been a most uncomfortable one because Hodgkiss had rebuffed all her efforts to discover the purpose of the trip.

And when they arrived he had placed a hand on her shoulder and told her to remain in the car.

When she protested he had insisted and said only that he had delicate matters to discuss with people at the club. He said he was not certain that the people concerned would even be there, but if they were it was better that she should not be present. 'Where ignorance is bliss 'tis folly to be wise,' he had quoted, maddeningly.

It was not the first time he had use this phrase and on previous occasions it had always turned out that her father had interviewed one or more witnesses in cases Donald was investigating at the time.

This in itself was alarming because the tranquility of the Burke household had been disturbed more than once when Donald discovered that Hodgkiss had taken an active role in one of his cases without bothering to see if his input would be welcome.

'Bloody interference,' he had called it on more than one occasion, although almost invariably the 'bloody interference' had brought the investigation to a successful conclusion.

Esme sighed. She turned on the car's radio and settled down to wait as her father strolled towards the club's entry.

In the wide, dim foyer Hodgkiss stopped and looked about. There was no one in sight. He crossed the room to examine an old painting of a steamboat, expertly executed but unsigned. The walls generally were decorated with photos and paintings of various boats, mostly power boats. Sailing boats appeared to be of no interest to the denizens of this place.

There was still no one in sight so Hodgkiss crossed to an unattended counter against a side wall. The counter was bare expect for an old fashioned brass bell with a large button on the top and beside it an ancient rather tatty book.

On the cover of the book Hodgkiss read in faded Italics *VISITORS.*

He opened the book and thumbed quickly through the pages. When he came to the most recent entries he paused, glanced around, took out a tiny notebook and a pencil and began writing.

He had closed the book and returned the notebook and pencil to his shirt pocket when a voice behind him inquired. 'Can I be of assistance, sir?'

Hodgkiss turned to see an elderly man dressed rather formally standing in an entry leading to what was obviously the club's bar.

'Can I get a drink here?' Hodgkiss asked. 'I'm not a member. Does that matter?'

'I'm afraid it does, sir. But if you sign our visitors' book, there on the counter in front of you, then I can have the pleasure of serving you a drink. Just sign your name in the column then I'll sign you in. I'm sure you know how it works.'

'I do indeed. A lot of unnecessary rigmarole,' he said, opening the book again. He turned to the last page and signed his name.

The other man ambled over to stand beside him. In the column next to where Hodgkiss had signed the man wrote Albert Hiskins.

He turned to Hodgkiss. 'Now, if you would be so good as to come through to my bar we'll see if we have what you want.'

'I'm sure you will,' said Hodgkiss, following.

Behind the bar Albert turned on Hodgkiss a practiced smile. 'Now, what will be your pleasure, sir?'

'Well, it may be a little disappointing but all I need is an orange juice with some ice in it.'

Albert nodded. 'Driving, are we?'

Hodgkiss shook his head. 'No. I've never driven in my life.

When I was a young fellow all my contemporaries could hardly wait to get get behind the wheel. Not me. I always thought it was much too risky. All that traffic rushing in all directions ... everyone mad as hatters and selfish as sin. All thought they owned the road. And that was forty years ago ... more.'

Albert smiled, pouring some orange juice from a plastic bottle into a glass with ice. 'And things have only got worse since then,' he said. 'Every day somewhere in the country there're poor people getting themselves killed and injured in spite of their seat belts and their radar traps.'

Hodgkiss said. 'I have a daughter. She drives. If I need to go somewhere a little off the beaten track she takes me there ... like today.'

'So our club is a little off your beaten track, is it, sir?'

'More than a little way off actually. My daughter used her phone to get us here, and I must say for a piece of modern technology it worked rather well.'

'Yes, my wife uses that too,' said Albert setting the drink down in front of Hodgkiss. 'Now, is there anything else, sir?'

Hodgkiss nodded. He had decided that Albert, while no doubt discreet, might nevertheless prove a source of information.

'Yes, there is something else. I understand there's a boat berthed here called the Trident?'

Albert nodded. 'The Trident. Yes. That's the Tracey's boat and a lovely old craft she is too. And beautifully maintained. If you go on board the Trident you take your shoes off first.

No shoes allowed on board. No exceptions. That's the only way to do it with a wooden boat, sir. Or that's Nola's view.'

'And I understand the owners of the Trident took a couple by the name of Connaught out on the river recently ... friends of theirs.'

Albert paused. He looked hard at Hodgkiss. 'Yes. They took the Connaughts out. But I would hardly have said they were friends.'

Apparently Albert was not quite so discreet as Hodgkiss had feared. 'I rather suspected that was the case,' he said, nodding wisely. 'There was a chill in the air between them ... something like that.'

'More than a chill,' said Albert. 'I've rarely seen such an oddly-assorted couple ... the women anyway. Nola, that's Mrs Tracey, is a real lady. And she loves the water. She turned up here ... last Wednesday was it .... yes ... with her husband, Gordon, and they waited out the front for these others to turn up. They were half an hour late and Nola was not happy. No one likes to be kept waiting, do they. I know I don't. But that was only the start of it. The other lady arrived all dresses up as if she as going to a Royal Garden Party.'

'Wearing the odd diamond or two, was she?' Hodgkiss asked.

'Much more than the odd diamond or two, I'm afraid,' said Albert. 'She was most inappropriately dressed for the water. And reading between the lines I rather gathered that the lady also gambled ... heavily and unsuccessfully.'

'Really,' said Hodgkiss. 'Rather a high-maintenance spouse then. I expect it must have been rather galling for the Tracey's, who I understand are not that well-off,' said Hodgkiss, taking a shot in the dark.

'Nola ... Mrs Tracey ... did not approve at all. Considered it all ostentatious ... bad taste.'

'Then I wonder why they invited them at all. Are they related perhaps?'

Albert shook his head. 'No. Not related, but Gordon was a great friend of the family. He used to do lot of work for James Connaught's father ... Gordon used to call him Old Mick. Rich as Croesus, or so I heard.'

'Then this James Connaught would have great expectations,' Hodgkiss speculated.

'They're more than just expectations now,' said Albert, polishing a glass vigourously. 'I understand the old gentleman ... Old Mick ... died very recently, and James will inherit.'

Hodgkiss asked. 'Do you think that has any connection to the very unlikely invitation for a trip on the river?

Albert put down the glass. 'Now that is a very interesting question, sir? Is there a particularly reason you asked it.'

Hodgkiss shrugged elaborately. 'The couples weren't particularly ... um compatible, you say. Everyone knows that the cost of maintaining a boat like the Trident is considerable, and the Connaughts recently came into money.'

Albert nodded. 'Yes, sir, I can see your drift.'

Hodgkiss leaned forward conspiratorially. 'But there is

something else … something you may not be aware of. The lady with the jewellery is no longer with us?'

'No longer with us?' Albert's eyebrows rose.

'Dead,' Hodgkiss explained. 'Probably murdered.'

Albert nodded. 'I can't say I'm surprised to hear it, sir. A most unpleasant lady. Not above provoking ill-will.'

'Have you actually heard her doing that … provoking ill-will?'

Albert shook his head. 'I'm not one to gossip about club matters, sir, and there was nothing actually said in my hearing, but it was fairly plain from Mr and Mrs Tracey's attitude after their guests had departed that they had been disappointed.'

'Disappointed?' Hodgkiss asked. 'Disappointed in what way?'

'Well, without actually betraying a confidence, and only reading between the lines, I would say that Mr Tracey … Gordon … had hoped that Mr Connaught might help with his present financial difficulties.'

'But I think you mentioned that they weren't great friends … the Connaughts and the Traceys?' Hodgkiss asked.

'Yes, that's true. But there was a little more to it than that. Over the years this gentleman, Old Mick, had given Mr Tracey tips on the stock marked in return for work he did around his property … a rather grand property I under-stand. I know this for a fact because Gordon sometimes passed these tips on to me, and although I did not invest myself I noticed that they almost always turned up trumps, so to speak. But from what I've gathered the latest tip was not at all sound and Gordon plunged rather too heavily and lost a great deal of money. Word around the club is that he may have to sell the Trident and even his home.'

'I see,' said Hodgkiss. 'So no doubt he felt that James Connaught might feel some duty to help, seeing it was his father who was the source of their problem. And did Mr Connaught agree to help?'

'I regret that he did not. Overtures were made during the course of the outing, but they were not successful.'

'So the display of jewellery must have been doubly galling for the Traceys.'

Albert nodded. 'It was particularly commented upon more than once, sir ... after the Connaughts had left, of course. I'd say that the lady's jewellery and her gambling, which I understand was mentioned during the boat trip, must have contributed to the strained atmosphere evident when they returned. And this murder ... Mrs Connaught. Have they found the person responsible?'

Hodgkiss shook his head 'Not yet. Actually it's my son-n-law, a detective inspector, who is conducting the investigation. He's not a terribly imaginative fellow, but he usually gets there in the end ... with a bit of assistance from time to time.'

'Assistance from yourself, would that be, sir?'

'It would,' Hodgkiss admitted.

'Then I hope, sir, that you won't take anything I've said about Mr and Mrs Tracey too much to heart. After all, this was a private conversation. They are a fine couple. Great assets to the club. We would really miss them.'

'You can put your mind at rest there,' said Hodgkiss, knowing that he would have to tell all this to Donald .... sometime.

He put down his empty glass.

'Another one, sir?' Albert asked hopefully.

'I'd love to,' said Hodgkiss, 'but my daughter is waiting in the car and she is not a particularly patient person. I think I had best be on my way.'

Esme was asleep when Hodgkiss returned to the car. He opened the door quietly and slid into his seat.

He had just settled, eyes closed thinking about Albert and their conversation when Esme asked. 'Well, Dad, home now, is it?'

'Yes, Esme, if you would be so good.'

When she started the motor Hodgkiss asked: 'Won't you need the phone to get us home?'

'I don't think so, Dad. I reckon I can find our way home from here.'

They had been traveling only a short while when Esme asked: 'Well, how did it go? Were they there ... the people you wanted to talk to?'

'No, but it didn't matter. I found out what I wanted to know ... or most of it.'

'Are you going to tell Donald? You should you know .... if it was about that dead body Sergeant Sanderson found in the bushes. I suppose it was, wasn't it?'

'Yes, Esme it was about her. And yes, I promise you I will pass on to Donald any useful information I have,' he said, turning to look his daughter in the eye.

But not necessarily straight away, he thought. There're one or two things I need to know first.

When Donald arrived home that evening Esme lost no time in informing him of Hodgkiss visit to the Buccaneers' Bay Cruising Club.

To Hodgkiss' surprise Donald took the news without rancour. 'So, Dad, what did you find out at this boat club? Anything interesting? Things I should know about?'

Hodgkiss shook his head. 'It was rather disappointing,' he said, which was not exactly true. 'The people I had hoped to see weren't there.' This was true, but in part only. He had hoped to identify the initials written in Phyllis Connaught's diary and this he had done from the visitors' book where Nola and Gordon Tracey had signed their names beside the names James and Phyllis Connaught.

But Hodgkiss felt no obligation to inform Donald of the interesting snippets of personal information provided by the talkative barman … not yet, anyway.

* * *

Benny's Uncle Ray was at his local when his phone, sitting on the bar beside him, rang. He glanced at the phone and was not pleased to see Detective Sergeant Frome's name on the screen.

Uncle Ray was in two minds about the call. His contacts

with the detective had at one time been fairly frequent and cordial. But that was before an unfortunate misunderstanding that was never properly resolved.

Detective Frome had been always pleased to receive calls from Uncle Benny who was the occasional source of interesting information about the inhabitants of the milieu in which he moved.

The sergeant was in no doubt about Uncle Ray's motives. Uncle Ray was not the least bit interested in smoothing the path of criminal justice or even boosting the detective's clear-up rate, although he assisted considerably in both. Benny's motives were purely self-interest. The information was passed on in the hope that it would cause serious embarrassment to competitors in whatever field he was working at the time.

Uncle Benny raised the phone cautiously and opened the connection.

'G'day there, Mr Frome,' he said cheerfully. 'Nice to hear from you,' he lied.

'Yeah. Long time, eh? Nothing much to talk to me about lately, eh?'

'Been living a quiet life here … in the suburbs. Nothing happens. The way I like it.'

'You must get bored shitless surely, a fellah like you. Always in the thick of things.'

'Not these days. Like I said … quiet … the way I like it.'

'Delighted to hear it, Ray. And how's your young Benny been behaving himself, eh?'

Uh Oh, thought Uncle Ray. Here it comes. What's the

little bugger been up to now. 'Don't see a lot of Benny these days,' he said, preparing for the worst.

'Pity,' said Detective Frome. 'I saw him the other day. Had a good long talk, we did.'

'That's nice,' said Uncle Ray, because he couldn't immediately think of anything else. 'Didn't know you knew him.'

'Oh yes. I know him. Actually I'd met him before once or twice. Not always helpful like his uncle.'

'Young people these days ...' said Uncle Benny, and left it at that.

'Yeah, not what they were in our days, eh?'

When Uncle Benny failed to pick up the conversation Detective Frome continued. 'You know that shaggin' wagon of his. You know ... the yellow one. Or is it violet. The eyes stop working when you've been looking at it for a while.'

'What's he done with it now?' Uncle Ray asked. 'Speeding I suppose. I told him when he bought the thing that it was too powerful and with that colour ... well you blokes weren't going to miss him, were you?'

'True enough, Ray, true enough. But it wasn't speeding we were chatting about. It was a bit worse than that.'

'Don't tell me he'd been drinking and driving. I warned him about that 'til I was blue in the face. If you've got to have a drink, I said ...'

'No, Ray, it wasn't drink-drive. Worse I'm afraid.'

'Not unregistered was he?. I told him that if he ever drove unregistered and had a prang ...'

'No. It was registered ... I think it was. But I might check just in case. It was worse than that anyway, and the wagon wasn't really the problem.'

'Then what's it about,' Uncle Ray asked, tired of guessing games.

'It's about murder, or manslaughter at best.'

'Murder. No, detective Frome.' Uncle Ray protested. 'You've got the wrong fellow … must have. Young Benny'd never murder anyone. He's not that sort of bloke. He's a good young bloke … basically.'

'Maybe, but it's not looking good.'

'What happened. What's it about?'

'That body they found out in the national park … just off Kanundda Head Road. Did you read about it. It was in the papers and bits on the tele.'

'News to me. So what did he have to do with it … if anything.'

'She was in the back of his wagon … the dead woman. No question. The forensic boys had a good look. Fibers from her clothes in a rug there … lots of other stuff. She was in the back of his wagon, no risk.'

'How old was she … I mean she wasn't a girl friend, was she? Couldn't have been because he's been going steady with this Fricka girl. She'd be furious if she knew Benny'd been two-timing her with this other piece. You'd really have a murder on your hands if she found out.'

'No. It was nothing like that. The dead woman was maybe 50 plus. And she hadn't had sex recently if that's any comfort to you.'

Uncle Ray decided it was time to mount a defense. But first he'd need a few facts. 'So what made you think of Benny in the first place.'

'It's that wagon of his,' said the detective. 'Once seen never forgotten. When the story about the dead woman came out we began getting calls. Lots of them, and all of them mentioned a brightly painted wagon on the spot where the body was first reported. You see what happened was that Benny moved the murdered woman's body from point A to Point B.'

Uncle Ray was trying to recall details of Benny's confused nocturnal phone call about finding a dead lady and what advice he had offered about moving her to some distant location to avoid identification.

From what Detective Frome had told him it seemed Benny had followed his advice but things had not gone according to plan.

But Uncle Ray could see no reason to over-load the detective with these details. 'But why would he do a thing like that? And besides, you haven't told me anything about this murdered woman. What happened? What's he supposed to have done to her?'

'The back of her head and a large rock came into violent contact … that's what happened to her. And she was in Benny's van shortly before it happened. But perhaps you've got a better explanation than him?'

'I haven't got any explanation. How could I? It's all news to me. But what did he say? He's an honest lad, you know. Basically.'

'I'll tell you what happened … not the story he told us, but what we've pieced together so far. Benny and his girlfriend were seen by a number of people carrying a women from the bush and putting her in the back of his wagon. There's no doubt about that. Four or five good witnesses. He drove off. Later we picked up his tyre tracks… and believe me they are just as obvious as his wagon … turning down into the bush a very short distance away. We know where he stopped and we saw shoes … probably his and hers … headed into the bush and back out again. No one saw them this time, or if they did they haven't rung in yet. But the forensic fellahs, who don't miss much, found a blood stain … her blood … on a ruddy great rock sticking out of the ground. The doctor said it was the rock that killed her which means that she was alive all the time Benny and his girlfriend were carting her around the countryside. Not very nice, Ray. Not very nice. Although there's one thing in his favour; at least he rang in and told us where to look for her. But even that wasn't much help to her since she was already dead.'

'So what happens now?' Uncle Ray asked. ' Did he ring a solicitor?'

'Said he didn't need one. Innocent people don't need them, he told me.'

'Sounds like Benny,' said Uncle Ray. 'Have you charged him with anything yet?'

'Yeah. Something about moving a dead body around without permission. Just to keep hold of him until they decide on the major charge.'

'But how's it going to be murder then? He didn't pick the rock up and brain her with it, did he?'

Detective Frome shook his head, clearly disappointed. 'No, actually they ruled that out. They reckoned rock was still firmly stuck in the ground. They reckon what must have happened was when they were carrying her from the wagon to put her in the bush they probably dropped her and her head hit the rock ... or something like that.'

'Well if that's all that happened they won't charge him with murder, will they. I mean, it was just an accident, right?' It could have happened to anyone.'

'I don't know about that,' said the detective, now beginning to feel that he was on the losing side of the argument. 'How many people d'you reckon go around in the bush in the middle of the night dropping dead bodies or even live ones.'

'OK. Then what about his girlfriend. What does she say about it? She must have been there. They always get around together.'

'Still looking for her,' said Detective Frome. 'He reckons he doesn't know where she is. Hasn't seen her since that night.'

'Well if that's what he said that'll be right. Brought up to tell the truth, that boy. But don't worry about her. She'll turn up. Always does. I'll ring and let you know next time I see her. You got the same number as before?'

'Yeah.'

*   *   *

James Connaught was amazed when a very agitated William Berger rang on the landline in his private office at home.

Before he could get a word out Berger gushed: 'Honestly James, I never thought you'd get around to it. I obviously misjudged you. I just heard about it on the radio. I can't thank you enough. You've really delivered … come through.'

James felt a wave of panic. What on earth was the man raving about. What did he think had happened. He had earnestly hoped that he would never hear from Berger or his wife again.

Last time they spoke had been after Phyllis disappeared. He had rung Berger and left a message on his phone and when Berger finally called back there had been a quite extraordinary conversation. In fact James had been left with the impression that Berger did not know what he was talking about and just wanted to get off the phone.

Now James had not the least idea what Berger was talking about, but after a moment's reflection he assumed that it must be about their arrangement. He improvised. 'I missed it on the radio. What did they say exactly?'

'Not a lot,' said William. 'Just that his body was found in his unit by a staff member who was concerned when he didn't turn up for work … that he'd missed a luncheon appointment and that it was a suspicious death and police are investigating. Nothing more. No details.'

'Good. Just as well, eh?' he said with an attempt to take charge of the conversation. 'Not like last time … the bloody footprint the killer left behind when Phyllis disappeared.'

'Bloody footprint.' William sounded alarmed.

'Yes,' said James. 'There wasn't any publicity about it at the time. No doubt the coppers think they can use it to trap whoever had been there and killed her. But we know they won't find anyone ... don't we?' An attempt at a conspiratorial chuckle.

James hurried on, anxious to end the confusing call, 'Look, thanks for calling to let me know it was on the radio, but remember, from now on there must be no contact between us. No phones, no emails .... nothing. The police mustn't be given any reason to suspect that there's ever been any connection between us ... right? I've never met you and you've never met me. That was always the guts of the arrangement. So goodbye and thanks for ringing to let me know it was on the radio. Now I'm going to wipe everything from this phone and if I can't do that I'll simply lose the thing or destroy it, and I suggest you do the same your end because if the coppers ever connects us we're in trouble. Agreed.'

'Agreed. Definitely,' said William. 'I'll destroy my phone too, if necessary. Good luck, James, and thanks again. It means a lot to have that bastard off my back permanently. Now with him gone I understand there might be a chance of us getting back in business with our shops.'

It had not yet occurred to either of them to ask the questions: who actually did the two killings and why?

* * *

Angela Bly did not have a jealous bone in her body. Which was just as well, because if it was otherwise she would have found working for Corey Wisdom something of a trial.

For Angela, twice married and twice divorced, her irregular and quite pleasurable dalliances with her employer where welcome diversions in a busy life. He was good company when he bothered to put himself out, and he paid her well to keep track of his business affairs.

His other affairs ... well, she simply did not concern herself with them. If he fancied some woman he saw, and pursued her, then good luck to him ... to them. He was big enough and old enough to take care of himself.

Sitting at her desk in the office outside Corey's suite, Angela glanced at the tiny diamond watch on her left wrist. It was ten o'clock.

Usually Angela was kept busy dealing with the routine problems that frequently arose from the running of one or other of the coffee shops in the chain.

Honestly, some of those managers wouldn't go to the bathroom without consulting her first.

But the matter now before her was one she would not decided without talking first to Wisdom. It related to the future of three of their coffee shops that had been particularly hard hit by the pandemic. The operators, William Berger and his wife, Esther, had written to Corey a very reasonable letter asking to have their rent suspended or reduced until the situation improved. It was not the first such letter they had received as many of their operators were experiencing similar problems due to the lock-downs, and usually Wisdom granted their requests with conditions.

So Angela was surprised when Corey told her to advise the Bergers in writing that he would not cut them any slack and that they must pay back rent immediately or vacate their shops.

She had suggested he comprise by reducing their rent and allowing time to pay arrears, the usual course when other operators had run into similar difficulties for the same reason.

But Corey had told her quite abruptly that when he wanted her advice he would ask for it, although she often gave advice gratis which usually was taken without discussion.

So Angela had decided that in the case of the Bergers there might be something personal behind Corey's refusal. But she knew of no reason for any personal animus.

When eleven o'clock came and Corey had still not appeared Angela rang the private phone he kept at the home unit. When it switched to the message bank she reminded him of a luncheon appointment at a nearby restaurant where he was a regular diner.

At one thirty the *maitre d'* of the restaurant rang to say that Mr Wisdom had not appeared and his guest was wondering if she should wait any longer. He explained that he had tried to contact Corey on his usual numbers without success.

Angela suggested the lady diner guest should either start her meal without him or perhaps put the present disappointment down to experience and wait to be asked on another date.

But Angela was becoming concerned. Corey's lifestyle, while irregular, was in many ways predictable. Rarely was he incommunicado as he was at the moment. He prided himself on his ability with technology. His skills with the computer matched her own and she had studied an advanced course.

So where on earth was the man? And why was he not answering his phones? And why had he stood up his luncheon date? Angela knew that he had been looking forward to today's lunch in particular. 'She is a most striking young woman,' he had told her. "I have great hopes for her.'

At five o'clock Angela put her computer to sleep and left the office. But before she left she took two keys from the top drawer of her desk and placed them in her handbag. These were the keys she would need to access the penthouse that Corey occupied in a low-rise block of units that Angela drove past twice a day on her way to and from work.

Perhaps she would call in just to satisfy herself that nothing was seriously amiss.

Probably she would find him in bed with some lady he had met at the gym he visited early every morning. If so she would not be the first lady gymnast who had come home with Corey to explore a different exercise routine.

As she approached the building she saw Corey's distinctive sports car parked around the corner from his flats. This was unusual. Every since some jealous vandal had scratched the car's duco while it was parked outside one of his coffee shops he always took steps, whenever possible, to leave it somewhere he could keep an eye on it unless the stay was to be only brief.

Angela parked opposite the building and crossed the road. She used one key to enter the building's foyer where a lift was waiting. She rode up to the fifth floor which Corey's unit shared with one other ... a mirror image of his.

Corey's unit, number twelve. was directly opposite the lift.

Angela used the second key to open the door.

'Mr Wisdom,' she called. 'I thought I'd drop by on my way home and see if everything was all right. I've had people ringing for you all day.'

When there was no reply she walked through to the large, minimally furnished living room at the front of the unit, but the room was empty.

Better try the bedroom, she thought.

Of course Angela knew where the master bedroom was located, having spent the night there herself on many occasions.

She tapped gently on the door. 'Anyone there?' she asked coquettishly.

When there was no response she turned the handle and pushed the door back.

Corey was there ... alone. But he was not in the extraordinarily large bed that stood directly opposite the door.

He was lying on the floor between the door to the en

suite bathroom and a second door that opened into the entry hall.

Angela hurried across the room and knelt on the deep pile carpet beside her employer, careful to avoid the blood stained area around the head.

She stood and reached for the phone in her handbag. Of course the ambulance and the police would have to be notified.

But she hesitated. Perhaps she should make a quick inspection of the unit first. Angela knew that there was a secret side to Wisdom's life; she thought of conversations suddenly suspended when she entered his office; papers turned over when she appeared ... locked drawers ... all manner of little furtive gestures that made her wonder exactly what else went on behind the scene of his rather traditional business life.

Then she saw the ring on the carpet beneath one of two identical bedside tables. It was certainly not a man's ring ... certainly nothing he would ever wear. There was a large emerald in the centre of the rose gold ring, and diamonds on the shoulders. It was a very expensive item.

Angela picked it up and slipped it on the middle finger of her left hand. She admired it. A very snug fit.

She decided the ring would be fair payment in lieu of the hours of unpaid overtime she had worked for Mr Wisdom, not to mention the other services she had provided for him gratis in this very room ... in this very bed.

Now, best call the ambulance and the coppers. She

stabbed a finger at the keypad of her phone.

She made the two calls, stating that the dead man was Corey Wisdom ... yes, she was certain because she had worked for him for several years ... then settled down to wait and to give thought to the unusual situation in which she found herself.

She decided that the woman who Wisdom had seen arguing with a man in the clearing on the night of their visit was her prime candidate for what happened here.

At Wisdom's request she had identified and located that woman, and later she had seen him looking on his computer at what she believed was the woman's home.

Yes, Corey had certainly shown more than a passing interest in her. But the question which now exercised Angela's mind was what should she say when the police arrived and began to investigate.

Should she volunteer information or follow the well-worn advice often proffered in legal circles to answer all questions as briefly as possible and leave it at that.

Yes. No point in making trouble for others unnecessarily. Who knows, she may need the woman they had seen in the clearing that night at some time. One never knew.

Besides, the police would soon discover the connection between that particular lady and Corey Wisdom when they examined his phone which lay, half hidden, under his body. No doubt they would find the numbers of several other ladies in his phone, but the police would be unwise to confine their inquiries to Corey's lady friends. There were several people associated with his coffee shops who would not mourn his passing.

She thought of the Bergers in particular.

And it was as if the thought had precipitated the event … her phone rang.

It was William Berger. As soon as he heard her voice Berger could scarcely contain his glee. 'Is it true, Angela? That he's dead. I just heard it on the radio. I don't dare believe it. They only said he was believed to be dead. Nothing confirmed officially.'

'You can believe it all right, although I must say the coppers didn't waste any time getting the news out. I told them only about ten minutes ago,' said Angela. 'But you needn't worry. He's dead. Very dead.'

'What on earth happened. Who did it? Do they know?'

'No. Early days yet. All I know is that he's lying dead on the floor near the ensuite. It looks like he fell and hit his head or some one hit it for him. I suppose I should be looking around for clues.'

'You mean like fingerprints or like the bloody footprint the murderer left at that Phyllis Connaught's place … you remember her, the lady who disappeared and was found dead later out in the national park?'

'No. I never head about a bloody footprint,' said Angela. 'Do you think the two deaths could be connected?'

'I've no idea,' said Berger quickly. 'That's all I know.'

Angela heard the sound of sirens approaching. 'Sounds like the coppers are arriving,' she said. 'I suppose I'll have to go and let them in.'

Angela cut the call, rose and hurried to the window in time to see two police cars stop outside the block.

She was surprised to see a large van bearing the logo of one of the local TV stations already parked opposite. Goodness, they lost no time getting here, she thought.

She was waiting at the unit's front door when the lift opened and two policemen stepped out. One, a tall man, bulky but not fat, wore an ill-fitting grey suit. The other presented a complete contrast; natty was the word Angela would have applied to him. A thin face but keen eyes. His suit was well pressed and fitted.

Both presented their credentials without a word and Angela read both quickly but thoroughly. The larger of the two men was detective Inspector Burke and the other was Detective Sergeant Sanderson.

Angela stood to one side. 'This way,' she said, then turned. 'Can I get you anything?'

'Not just now, thank you,' said Detective Burke. 'Later perhaps.'

Then. 'Was it you who rang the station?'

'Yes,' said Angela.

'Then it was you who found the … him?'

She nodded. 'Do you need me to stay? I have things to do right now, obviously.'

Detective Burke turned sharply. 'I dare say you have, but I'll need a statement from you before you go anywhere.' He turned to the other detective then back. 'Sergeant

Sanderson will take it shortly if that's convenient for you.'

'Of course,' said Angela. 'The sooner the better. You'll find me in the kitchen.'

She had just finished her second cup of coffee, made with the complicated machine on the long marble bench under the window, when Sergeant Sanderson appeared in the doorway, notebook in one hand and a multi-coloured vintage fountain pen in the other.

The sergeant asked: 'If you have a moment, there are one or two things I'd like to ask …'

'A coffee first, perhaps sergeant?' she asked.

The sergeant nodded. 'If it's not too much trouble.'

'No trouble at all,' said Angela, turning to the machine.

Soon they were settled across from each other at the large island bench in the centre of the room.

'Now if you wouldn't mind answering just one or two questions.'

'Not at all,' said Angela. 'I'm happy to help in any way I can,' she said, realising with surprise that this was exactly true. She knew there was nothing about her relationship with Corey Wisdom she needed to hide from this police-man or from anyone. She could think of no consequences to be faced by telling the truth about her working relationship with Wisdom. She knew exactly how the chain of coffee shops operated and she knew Corey Wisdom had no reason to cut corners in his business dealings.

Other aspects of his life, his love-life in particularly, well no doubt the police would nose out details of that in due course without her help.

As for their personal relationship ... well, that would be certain to come out anyway, so she would talk about that up front.

Sergeant Sanderson sipped his coffee, put it down carefully and began.

The first question was the one Angela had been expecting. 'Can you think of anyone who might have wished to harm Mr Wisdom?'

Angela had decided not to throw the Bergers under the bus by telling the policeman about their problem with Wisdom and thus put them in the position of prime candidates for the role of first murderers. She had some sympathy for the Bergers' dilemma. Anyway, the police would soon learn of their problem when they went through Wisdom's emails.

Angela thought there were others more deserving of a audition for the role of murderer.

She began. 'Well, officer, I think it would be fair to say that Corey Wisdom is ... was ... what some people would call a pants man.'

She was surprised to see a blush wash over the sergeant's face. Goodness, how does such innocence survive to the rank of sergeant, she wondered.

She added. 'And if you decide to make a list of his lady friends you should include my name.'

The blush made a second appearance.

Then began the process of taking the statement which was not at all what Angela had come to expect from watching police dramas on the television.

Very few of the sergeants on television were as conscientious as Sergeant Sanderson. After each question the sergeant was at great pains to write her entire response verbatim.

It was a tedious process. During the gaps while Sergeant Sanderson wrote in his pad Angela noticed white-clad figures, all with large floppy white foot-coverings, coming and going in the hallway outside the kitchen.

At one point Inspector Burke put his head around the door. 'How's it going, Sergeant,' he asked. 'Nearly finished?'

Sergeant Sanderson replied. 'Yes, inspector. Just another question or two.'

This turned out to be an answer that gave Angela a false hope. It was twenty minutes before Sargent Sanderson closed his note book, screwed the cap back on his pen and replaced it in his shirt pocket.

'Thank you for your assistance, Ms Bly,' he said, straight faced.

At the door he stopped and turned. 'Nice ring you're wearing. Do you mind telling me where you got it?'

'Not at all,' said Angela. 'A friend gave it to me …. not Mr Wisdom if you were wondering.'

Angela cursed silently. You're a bloody fool, she told herself. Now you'll have to find someone willing to back up your lies. Still, what are friends for?

But apparently the sergeant had not finished. 'Your phone, Ms Bly … I'll need to take your phone.'

Angela feigned surprise. 'My phone, sergeant ... whatever do you want with my phone?'

The sergeant replied dead-pan. 'Just routine, Ms Bly. 'I'm sure we won't need to keep it for long.'

Angela took the phone from her handbag and handed it to the sergeant. 'As soon as you can, please. It's like having a part of me amputated.'

As soon as the sergeant had gone Angela hurried through to the room which Wisdom sometimes used as an office. She pulled open a drawer and took out a tiny blue phone. She searched through the phone briefly then dialed. Moments later a woman's voice answered cautiously.

Angela asked. 'Mrs Tracey, is it?'

A deep female voice, tinged with anxiety, asked: 'Who wants to know?'

Angela felt considerable sympathy for the woman. 'My name is Angela Bly. I'm Corey Wisdom's secretary. You haven't lost a ring have you? Very recently? Nice ring ... very expensive I'd say.'

'No.' The answer was definite.

Angela continued. 'Because if you have don't worry about it. I'm at Corey's place now and the police are buzzing around like bluebottles.'

She paused. 'I suppose you've heard about it, have you ... what happened to Corey?'

'Yes, I heard it on the radio just now. It didn't say much though. Just that he was found by one of his staff. Was that you?'

'Yes, it was.'

'Must have been very unpleasant? There were no details about what actually happened … how he died.'

'Well there were no bloody footprints like in the bedroom of that woman they found out in the national park. I know that much.'

'Do you mean that Mrs Connaught?' Nola asked.

'Yes, I think that was the woman's name.'

'I didn't hear anything about a bloody footprint.'

'I don't think the police mentioned it … probably on purpose. Keeping quite about it so they can catch the killer off guard I dare say. I've only just heard about it.'

There, now the woman will probably think I've just heard about it by talking to the coppers working here now.

She continued. 'But there was nothing like that happened here. From what I saw when I arrived, and by hanging around at doors listening to them talking, I think the story is that someone gave him a good whack on the head … and that was it. End of Mr Wisdom.'

'And who do they think did it? Any ideas?'

'Not a one … not that I've heard. I had to make a statement but of course I couldn't tell them much. He was well and truly dead when I arrived and I don't mind telling you that although I worked for him I was not a great fan. He never hesitated to use people for his own profit or amusement … women in particular.'

'Not wrong there,' Nola muttered, more to herself.

Angela continued with emphasis. 'Now, there is one thing

in particular I think you ought to know … that is apart from that footprint. I think it's likely that your phone number will appear in Corey's phone for sometime today. I dare say that may not be the only time it appears, but you'd know about that. But about the call today … it occurs to me that it might be as well if you had a good story ready for the police.'

She cut the connection without waiting for a reply, then slipped the phone into a pocket.

Now I suppose I'll have to dump this phone because if the coppers get their hands on it they'll want to know who used it after Corey was dead …. and why. These bloody phones. There's no such thing as privacy with them.'

*   *   *

Hodgkiss always knew when Donald was struggling with an investigation. Too proud to ask directly for help, Donald's approach would be circuitous … but demanding nevertheless.

If Hodgkiss was sitting reading in one of the wingback chairs in the family room with his back to the light, or slumped in one of the uncomfortable director's chair on the back deck studying the chess problem, Donald would approach … sit nearby … and say nothing.

It would always be left to Hodgkiss to open the conversation.

As it was now.

Hodgkiss had just found the key to the chess problem …

another waiting move with the white king … when Donald pushed back the sliding door from the family room and stepped out to the deck. He slumped heavily on the curved bench opposite, vented an exaggerated grunt of anguish designed to catch Hodgkiss' attention, then retreated into a pointed silence.

Hodgkiss recognised the symptoms immediately.

One look at Donald's face told the story. Written there clearly were all the signs of anguish and frustration that always appeared when one of his investigations was not going according to plan and he had reached the point where he recognised that help must be sought if progress was to be made.

Hodgkiss knew there was no point in further prolonging the silence which had now stretched into a third minute. They could sit like this for the rest of the day and Donald would say nothing that could possibly be construed as a plea for help.

'So how's it going?' Hodgkiss asked brightly. 'Any progress on the death of that woman they found in the Kanundda National Park … the one whose body Sergeant Sanderson said had been moved?'

Donald grunted and shook his head. 'Nice if that was the only case I had to work on. I'd probably have had it tidied up by now.'

Hodgkiss took the hint. 'Oh? What's happened? Has Superintendent O'Hare put you on another case?'

Donald nodded gloomily. 'I wouldn't mind if it was

another case, but now I've got two cases running at once ...
two murders. As if one isn't enough.'

'So what's the new case?' Hodgkiss asked obligingly.

'It's that bloke found dead in his penthouse .... the Coffee
Shop King they called him. Corey Wisdom.'

Hodgkiss had heard a garbled report of Wisdom's death
on the early news. 'And why did Mr O'Hare hand you that
case as well as the woman ... what was her name ... Phyllis
Someone, wasn't it?'

'Connaught. He reckons they're connected ... Mrs
Connaught and this Wisdom guy.'

'Connected how? What made him think that?'

'When we went through Wisdom's phone we found he'd
written down a couple of cars' numberplates and one of
them was the numberplate of the Connaught woman's car
... and he'd actually entered it on his phone on the night she
died and probably about the right time too. It'd be nice if he
was still around to tell us something about it; why he did it.
I mean, he must have had a reason.'

Hodgkiss asked. 'No doubt. I suppose you've spoken to
the woman's husband, have you? What did he know about
this Wisdom fellow?'

'Yeah, I spoke to him just now. He reckons he didn't know
the fellow from Adam, and if his wife knew him she never
said anything to him about it. But he thinks it's pretty
unlikely that she knew him. She doesn't even drink coffee.'

'And what about him? Where was he at the time?'

'No problem there,' said Donald. 'He was at his chess club

until midnight.'

'So does that give him an alibi for her murder?'

'Not necessarily. We still haven't got a precise time of death for her yet. And I guess moving her might have confused things a bit.'

'Well, Donald, I think you can safely conclude that the late Mr Wisdom did not take the trouble to copy the lady's numberplate into his phone in the middle of the night on a whim. As it stands it is proof that he and Mrs Connaught … both now deceased … were present at this rather remote spot at the same time. It certainly requires explanation. Now, as I recall when she disappeared a lot of valuable jewellery disappeared with her. Has any of that come to light as yet?'

Donald shook his head. 'Not so much as an earring. All the pawnbrokers have got photos of the stuff but nothing's turned up so far.'

'And any progress yet on finding whoever moved her body?'

Again Donald shook his head. 'Nah, and I won't be wasting too much time on that. Chances of finding who moved her aren't too good. Car tracks everywhere. Busy place that.'

'Anything else of interest on Wisdom's phone?'

'Only the other car numberplate and nothing much of interest there. The car was registered to a Mr Gordon Tracey. Where he comes into the picture I've no idea. Sanderson asked him what he was doing there and he came up with a lot of nonsense about him and his wife liking to go there when they were in a romantic mood. They used to go there a lot before they were married ... "when we were courting" is what he told Sanderson. Apparently they're the kind of people who think it's more enjoyable to do things in their car rather than in a bed like normal civilized people.

'I've told Sanderson to follow up on that if he hasn't already because I don't believe a word of it.'

If Donald had not been distracted by a colourful bird alighting on the wooden rail around the deck he would have noticed the look of surprise fleet across his father-in-law's face.

Hodgkiss recalled in some detail what Albert the barman at the Buccaneers' Bay Cruising Club had to say about the Tracey's and their day on the water with the Connaughts, but he decided not to burden Donald with the knowledge since he appeared to be already struggling with information overload.

But it was a connection which he would have to pursue ... and soon.

'And who found the body ... Wisdom's?' he asked.

'A woman who works for him,' said Donald. 'Angela Bly. She reckoned he'd been out of the office all day and no one had been able to contact him. He'd missed meetings and a lunch engagement. She was just wondering where he was and what he was up to. She had a key to his place and went in and found him.'

Hodgkiss asked. 'So she had a key to his place? Why was that?'

'Sanderson said this Wisdom apparently had a lot of

girlfriends ... and she was one of them ... thus the key. She didn't mind admitting it. Besides she often worked from there.'

'And how did he die?'

'He hit his head on the corner of a marble table in the main bedroom.

'"He hit his head", Hodgkiss quoted. 'Or do you mean someone hit his head?'

Donald shrugged. 'A bit hard to say yet although there were a few little areas of bruising on his forearm as if someone had tried to hold on to him. Anyway the doctor said the hit on the head knocked him out but it wasn't that that killed him.'

'So what did?'

'Someone strangled him with a belt ... probably one of his own belts. He had a few of them hanging up in a cupboard in his bedroom.

'So it probably wasn't planned if the killer didn't bring the weapon with him.'

'That'd be a pretty safe guess.'

'And from what you've told me a woman could have done it?'

'Yes. And if you're wondering if he'd had sex before he died the answer is yes. Very soon before he died.'

'Fingerprints?'

'Plenty of them but nothing useful yet.'

'And this Ms Bly ... how did she strike you? A reliable witness would you say?'

Donald shrugged. 'Yeah. Sanderson took her statement. Said she came across as pretty straight forward. Didn't balk at answering any of his questions. Didn't seem too upset at him dying either. The sort of woman who'd probably have no trouble landing another job. Or that's what he thought of her.'

Hodgkiss nodded. 'Competent. Maybe competent enough to arrange a murder and get away with it.'

Donald shook his head. 'D'you reckon? Nice if it was that easy.'

Hodgkiss asked. 'Did you happen to bring home any of the statements Sergeant Sanderson has taken in the matter?'

'Yes. Why? Do you want to read them? If so you'll need a spare two hours. You know how he takes statements.'

'Yes, Donald, I am well aware of the sergeant's rather pedantic practices. Nevertheless I may find something worth pursuing. I think it is fair to say that I have in the past.'

Donald pushed back from the table. 'OK, Dad. You asked for it. They're in my briefcase.'

He disappeared inside and returned moments later with a fat folder. He slammed it down on the table in front of his father-in-law 'Good luck with that,' he said. 'Let me know if you find anything interesting that I haven't already told you about.'

Hodgkiss opened the folder and began reading.

He was still crouched over the file, glasses on the tip of his nose, when Donald reappeared an hour later. 'Well,' he asked. 'Find anything?'

Hodgkiss looked up. 'Two things,' he said. 'Sanderson mentioned that Wisdom's secretary, Ms Bly, was wearing a rather expensive looking ring. Do we know whether or not this was part of the jewellery stolen from the late Mrs Connaught?'

Donald shook his head. 'No. And we've got no reason to believe that it is. She said a friend gave it to her.'

'Did she specify the friend?'

Donald shrugged. 'Doesn't it say who it was in Sanderson's transcript?'

Hodgkiss shook his head.

'Then she wouldn't have said who gave it to her or Sanderson would have put it in. And what was the other thing you wanted to know?'

'Why did Superintendent O'Hare think the two murders were connected?'

Donald shook his head. 'No reason really. I asked him the same question but all he could say was it was just a feeling he had.'

'So you mistrust the superintendent's instincts do you, Donald?'

Donald shrugged. 'I've got enough on my plate without spending more time following up on Mr O'Hare's hunches. I can tell you now that there's no connection between most of the people involved in this business. Of course we know about Wisdom and the girl who found him ... she works for him. No big mystery there. But the Connaughts had nothing to do with Wisdom.'

Hodgkiss held up a hand. 'One moment there, Donald. I disagree. Wasn't the registration number of Mrs Connaughts vehicle recorded on Wisdom's phone?'

Donald thought. 'Yes, you're right. But we don't know why he bothered to take it down, do we?'

'No. But don't you think it would be a good idea to find out?'

'Find out how? The man's dead ... and so's the woman. Remember?'

'You could ask the the dead lady's husband ... James, isn't it? He might have some idea.'

'He's already been interviewed and according to him he was at his chess club at the time.'

'Yes, but was he still there when Wisdom recorded the vehicle's number on his phone? Do we know that? Sanderson has said nothing about that in any of the material I've read so far. It could still show a connection between Wisdom and the Connaughts.'

'And what if it did? Why would the Connaughts want to kill Wisdom. They didn't even know each other. It's there in the statement James Connaught made.'

Hodgkiss nodded patiently. 'Yes, Donald, I read that. However at this stage in the investigation I am not prepared to take as gospel everything the suspects told Sanderson.'

'Suspects?' Donald exclaimed. 'So you think James Connaught is a suspect, do you? Which murder ... his wife's or Wisdom's.'

'Donald, please do not make fatuous remarks. His wife's

of course. And you cannot exclude him until we know her precise time of death and where he was then.'

Donald nodded. 'OK, Dad. I'll get Sanderson on to it first thing tomorrow.'

'What's wrong with now. The more time you allow these people the more chance they have to cover their tracks. And another thing ... that bloody footprint found at the Connaughts. Anything there?'

'No, Dad. And there's not likely to be until we find some likely person with a foot we can compare it with.'

'Did the scientific people say whether or not it was a male or female footprint?'

'They couldn't say for sure but going on the size they thought it was most likely to be a woman's.'

Hodgkiss nodded 'Very well, Why don't you visit all the women connected with the two cases and ask to see their feet?'

Donald's jaw dropped. 'Dad. You have to be joking. We can't go around asking people to show us their feet?'

'Why ever not? You take fingerprints. People have to make their hands available. Why not their feet?'

'We have to have very good reasons before we can take anyone's fingerprints. We can't just rock up and take them whenever we feel like it. Nice if we could. Besides, how many women d'you reckon are involved in this business?'

'I would say there are two at least; first the secretary, Ms Bly and secondly, the lady, who together with her husband, Mr Wisdom had unreasonably depriving of their living by evicting them from their business, according to the emails Sanderson found on Wisdom's computer.'

'And these are the two whose feet we should be examining. Is that what you reckon?'

'Yes, I think it would be worthwhile even if only to exclude them from the Connaught murder.'

'Anything else you think I ought to do? I suppose you think I ought to be examining the feet of all the women who work in any of Wisdom's coffee shops, perhaps?'

'Really, Donald, sarcasm does not suit you at all,' said Hodgkiss.

But there was another matter which Hodgkiss knew he would have to mention ... his visit to the Buccaneer's Bay Cruising Club. He had hitherto avoided mentioning it for fear of raising Donald's ire at what he would no doubt see as another example of him meddling in one of his investigations.

Hodgkiss turned his attention once more to the bundle of documents Donald had left and found, buried in the mountain of Sanderson's papers, a short not saying —

Albert Hiskins, an employee of the Buccaneer's Bay Cruising Club has called saying he has some information that may be of assistance in relation to the death of Mrs Connaught which he heard about on the radio. I have not yet contacted him with the view of conducting an interview. I await your instructions on this. Personally I do not see how it can be connected with our investigations.

He looked up at Donald who was still seated opposite.

'There is a third woman I think it would be as well for you to interview, Donald,' he began.

'Oh, and who's that?'

'The lady who, together with her husband, was in the Lover's Lane area at the same time as Connaught and Mr James. Her husband's vehicle number was also among those noted on Wisdom's phone. A Mrs Tracy I think her name is.'

'And why should we bother with her. What's she got to do with it?'

'She was in the vicinity. Isn't that reason enough?'

'No. Going by all the tyre tracks in the area half of Sydney was in and out of that place around the time Mrs Connaught's body was dumped there.'

Hodgkiss decided he had said enough to cover himself. If Donald refused to take his advice then ... well, Donald couldn't blame him if it turned out that Mrs Tracey had played some part in Mrs Connaught's demise ... something that seemed to Hodgkiss at least a possibility considering the ill-will that existed between the two women, according to Albert.

And one of the causes of the ill-will was undoubtedly the array of jewellery which Mrs Connaught had displayed that day at the club.

Then there was the valuable ring of dubious provenance being worn by Mr Wisdom's secretary, Ms Bly, which Sanderson had noted.

What were the possible connections there?

If Sanderson pressed Ms Bly on the question of who gave

her the ring and the lady was still not forthcoming then perhaps it should be compared with the list of jewellery Mr Connaught had submitted to his insurance company.

If the ring matched the description of any of the items on the list that would raise some very interesting questions and possibly establish some unlikely connections between the parties.

Hodgkiss was becoming more and more convinced that Superintendent O'Hare was right in sensing connections between the two murders.

It was the motives that were still unclear.

No doubt the Bergers would not have been distressed to learn of Mr Wisdom's death, but there was absolutely nothing to connect them with the events leading to it.

While there had been many contacts, mostly emails, between the Bergers and Wisdom, there was still nothing that could in any way connected them to Mrs Connaught's death.

Certainly Sergeant Sanderson's round of interviews had failed to reveal any such connection.

Yet somehow Hodgkiss felt, quite unreasonably, that the superintendent's instinct was right and that some connection would eventually appear between the Bergers and the events surrounding Wisdom's death.

If Donald did not follow his suggestion to take closer look at Mrs Tracey ... and from all reports she was worth looking at ... then it was no longer his problem.

He said. 'Very well, Donald, I have given you my advice.

You can take it or leave it. It is a matter or no concern to me.'

He picked up the chess problem, and the bundle of papers, pushed back the bench and headed inside. At the door he stopped and turned. 'But I am firmly of the view that the Traceys are worth looking at, Donald.

'Why not ask Sanderson what he thinks,' he added.

* * *

Sergeant Sanderson was feeling anxious. Very anxious.

But anxiety was a normal state of mind with the sergeant. It was a condition stoked by working with Inspector Burke. Not that the inspector was an unreasonable man. It was just that he was acutely conscious of Mr Burke's impatience with some of his methods ... taking witness statements in particular.

The sergeant felt that in this matter he had a duty to record as accurately as possible every word spoken by a witness since the words he recorded could have a very significant bearing on the future of some person who he may not have met or even heard of.

But because the sergeant did not write shorthand, and since his longhand, while perfectly legible, was not speedy, the process was usually very time-consuming. And the inspector did not like his time being consumed unreasonably when he was working on a difficult case and felt under pressure... as he did at present.

Thus the sergeant was always looking for ways to convince Inspector Burke that he was thoroughly up to the task.

In this he had been assisted more than once by the inspector's father-in-law, Mr Hodgkiss. On occasions Sergeant Sanderson found himself torn between the wish to remain loyal to his inspector and his desire to pursue the advice offered by Mr Hodgkiss since he had concluded that Mr Hodgkiss had a definite talent for solving crime ... and not just the run-of-the-mill crimes that came along, but the very baffling cases that had stumped the inspector and sometimes the superintendent.

Hodgkiss talent had manifest itself many times and in some quite surprising ways during the time that Sanderson had come to know him. At first he had thought of Hodgkiss as 'that old gentleman,' not that he was really a gentleman in the literal sense of the word. Nor very old.

There was certainly nothing gentlemanly in the way he sometimes treated the inspector. He had seen his superior almost reduced tears, tears of frustration, on the odd occasion when he had been present at consultations between the two. It had been so embarrassing. Hodgkiss made no bones of his utter contempt for the inspector's failure to see things which Hodgkiss described as 'obvious' but which Sanderson, too, had overlooked.

On more than one occasion Mr Hodgkiss had provided him with information that he, in turn had passed on to the inspector ... information that almost always had turned out to be very valuable indeed. And Mr Hodgkiss did not mind at all if he took credit for these happy outcomes.

And the sergeant knew that Inspector Burke could not reasonably object to his contacts with Mr Hodgkiss since he had on occasions, admittedly not often, suggested that he contact Hodgkiss on particular matters.

Now Mr Hodgkiss had contacted him.

He had offered the suggestion that it may be productive if he made contact with the barman at some remote club that the sergeant had never heard of. Once there he should pursue a particular line of questioning about events that took place there on a certain day, events involving Mrs Phyllis Connaught ... the dead lady in one of the cases they were working on at present ... her husband, James, and a couple by the name of Tracey ... Gordon and Nola Tracy.

Mr Hodgkiss had suggested that he might mention this in one of his various reports to the Inspector.

Sergeant Sanderson had done this and was awaiting results.

He had not long to wait. The phone in his jacket pocket rang. He took it out and glanced at the screen. It was the inspector ... right on cue.

As is so often the case with such calls he had no idea where the inspector was at the moment. He could be out somewhere interviewing witnesses or even making an arrest; or he could be at home for lunch, or here at the station somewhere.

'Yes, sir?' said Sanderson.

'Sergeant. I want you to go to a place called the Buccaneer's Bay Cruising Club. Every heard of it? God alone knows where it is, but you'll find it on your phone no doubt.

'While you're there you should find a barman by the name of Albert. Have a word with him. He might know something about Mrs Connaught. Apparently she visited there shortly before she got killed. OK? Went out on a boat with another couple ... might be locals. Have a look at it and let me know if you hear anything worthwhile, but I'm not holding my breath.'

'I'll get onto it right away, Inspector,' said the sergeant, relieved that the inspector had not suspected his father-in-law's hand in the matter.

He consulted a telephone directory for the address of the club then entered into the phone.

No more thank an hour's easy drive, he calculated.

*   *   *

While the sergeant drove, alert to the occasional words of advice from his phone, the object of his trip, Albert Hiskins, was standing on the front verandah of the Buccaneer's Bay Cruising Club.

Albert knew from long experience that few if any members would turn up before lunch so he had decided to enjoy some sunshine.

And there was always the possibility that Nola Tracey might turn up to brighten his day ... days he thought of as

Nola Days.

There had been one such day a little earlier in the week.

Nola had arrived without her husband, Gordon, which was in itself a little unusual. She had seemed subdued rather than her usual bright and breezy self.

And the reason for this had soon become evident.

A very loud fellow driving a very loud motor car had arrived at the club shortly after Nola ... by arrangement, Albert had concluded.

They had come to his bar and he had served them drinks. The man had taken his drink to a table in the far corner of the room with Nola following.

Even from that distance Albert could tell from the couple's body language that it was not a pleasant meeting.

The man was leaning forward aggressively, both elbows on the table in what could have been described as a threatening manner, while Nola was leaning back in her chair as if trying to put as much distance as possible between herself and the fellow.

And he was doing most of the talking in a voice not quite loud enough to reach the bar, although the occasional word was audible.

Among these words were at least two that gave Albert a clue to the drift of the conversation: 'boat' and 'jewellery.'

These words were enough to turn Albert's thoughts to the day recently when Nola and Gordon had taken that couple out on the river; the fellow and his wife who had been murdered not long afterwards ... the woman who had turned up decked out in the most inappropriate jewellery for a day on the river.

But what did this loud, obnoxious fellow have to do with it all, Albert wondered.

The man came across to the bar and ordered another round of drink and immediately returned with them to the table and the intense conversation had resumed.

About ten minutes later the man had got up and left the bar without a word. No thank you and no tip. Moments later Albert heard his car depart noisily.

Then Nola had carried the empty glasses back to the bar where Albert had another drink ready for her.

'Rather loud sort of fellow … bit like his car,' Albert had commented by way of starting a conversation.

But Nola had merely nodded miserably.

Then Albert noticed that the beautiful emerald ring that Nola had been wearing on the middle finger of her left had when she arrived had gone.

Surely that fellow had taken it. There could be no other explanation. He had noticed it in particular. Indeed you could scarcely miss it. Albert was certain that he had not seen her remove it and give it to the man. But then he was not watching them at every moment.

That must have been why he came here, he thought; to bully the poor girl into handing over the ring. But why on earth had she agreed. He knew … indeed the whole membership knew … that the Tracey's were not terribly well off. But to simply hand over something like that to a type who

Albert regarded with grave suspicion ... well, that would require some explanation. Unless of course they had been forced to sell it to raise money for some urgent purpose.

But Albert was not satisfied with that explanation. He sensed something more sinister.

And as he stood on the verandah turning over the disturbing incident in his mind a dark sedan turned in off the road into the club's parking area.

It stopped, the driver's door opened and the driver stepped out. There was something about the car, the man, his clothes and his deportment that left Albert in no doubt about his occupation; he was a plainclothes copper.

'Yes, sir,' said Albert as the man approached. 'Can I help you?'

As if to confirm Albert's speculation the man draw an identity folder from an inner pocket and held it out for inspection; Detective Sergeant Sanderson.

'Just a couple of questions if you wouldn't mind?' the sergeant said.

'Then come inside and we can be more comfortable. But first things first, sir; the visitors' book.'

Albert led Sergeant Sanderson across the entry lobby to a counter where a large old fashioned book rested.

Albert opened the book and thumbed through the pages. 'Just here, sir, if you would like to sign in the column,' said Albert offering a biro.

The sergeant reach into his jacket and came out with a colourful fountain pen. He unscrewed the cap and signed his name with a flourish in the column and Albert signed with the biro in the adjacent space.

'Now if you'd care to step this way, sir,' said Albert heading off towards the bar.

But he had not gone far before he realised that the sergeant was not following him. He turned and looked back. The sergeant appeared to be busy copying material from the visitors' book into a small notebook. And not just the odd name or two. The sergeant seemed interested in the details of visitors in previous days and weeks.

Albert saw the detective close the notebook and return it and the pen to a jacket pocket. 'Coming now,' he called.

'Can I give you something to drink, sir?' Albert asked.

'You can't *give* me anything, Mr Hiskins,' said the detective with the trace of a smile. Then he added. 'But of course that's not what you meant to say, was it?'

'It was not, sir,' said Albert. 'Now, a beer perhaps. Or something a little stronger, is it?'

'Or perhaps something not strong at all ... not while I'm on duty,' said Sanderson.

'Off course, sir. Orange juice?'

'Perfect,' said the sergeant, looking around the empty room.

'Most people come for dinner ... not lunch,' said Albert. 'We often have quite a crowd for dinner, particularly at weekends. Mostly members and their friends.'

'I see you had a Mr Wisdom here recently. A visitor. Was that for dinner?'

'No. He only stopped in for a drink.' Albert did not want to talk about Mr Wisdom or his visit or what had happened.

But the sergeant continued. 'And I noticed he was signed in by someone ... I suppose it would have had to be a member, but I couldn't read the signature. Might have been a doctor. You wouldn't remember who it was, would you? If you don't remember perhaps you'd have a look in the book and read it for me. I'm sure you'd know all your members' signatures.'

'I wouldn't be too sure of that. Why? Is it important? Our people are very privacy conscious.'

'It's part of a police investigation, I wouldn't ask if it wasn't important.'

'Then without looking at the book I'm pretty sure it was Mrs Tracey who signed Mr Wisdom in that day' said Albert.

'Did Mrs Tracey know this Wisdom fellow?'

'A member doesn't have to know the person they're signing in. I signed you in, didn't I and I don't know you from Adam.'

'No. But you didn't answer my question, Mr Hiskins. Did Mrs Tracey know Mr Wisdom. Do you know, or did he just arrive here and she happened to be conveniently around to sign him in.'

'Yes, she happened to be here at the time.'

'But you could have signed him in, couldn't you? You signed me in.'

'Yes, I suppose I could have, but she just happened to be there when he got here.'

119

'You mean she was waiting there for him to arrive ... waiting out in the foyer ?'

Albert did not like the way this conversation was going. 'No. I don't mean that at all.'

'Very well. Then can you tell me this; what did Mr Wisdom do after Mrs Tracey signed him in? I suppose he had a drink did he, or was it lunch time and he went to the dining room?'

'No. They ... he was too early for lunch. It was only about ten o'clock when he got here.'

Sanderson nodded towards the cash register that stood at one end of the bar. 'I suppose there'd be records, wouldn't there, of the price of any drinks the fellow bought. I mean, that's what cash registers are for isn't it. To keep records. You could easily have a look and tell me what drinks you sold around ten o'clock that day. Right?'

'Yes, sir. No doubt that would be possible. But if you insist that I ferret out that sort of confidential information I'm quite sure the club secretary, who is responsible for finances, and the management committee would wish to be consulted first. They may not agree. As I said, sir, members are very conscious of their privacy.'

Sanderson shook his head. 'I wouldn't want to bother the secretary or the committee over these sort of details, and I'm sure you wouldn't either. So perhaps, if you think about it for a moment, you might be able to tell me, off the top of your head, and without bothering anyone, exactly what drinks you served between, say, ten and eleven on that day.'

'I really do not think I could do that, sir. It would not be proper.'

'Not proper!' Sergeant Sanderson exclaimed. 'Really, Mr Hiskins, if you continue to deny knowledge of anything that happened here in the bar around that time I will be tempted to think that something untoward or even illegal took place.'

Now Albert was becoming quite flustered. 'I'm quite certain that nothing of that sort took place.'

Sergeant Sanderson pressed on. 'I'm very relieved to hear that, Mr Hiskins. Now, since it was only a few days ago you must be able to remember what happened. Mrs Tracey is well-known to you, is she not? We know that she met Mr Wisdom in the foyer where she signed him in to the club. Now, what happened after that? Did she accompany him here to the bar? Did you serve her with a drink? Did you have a drink too? Did they stand here at the bar drinking? Did they talk to each other? Did they talk to you perhaps? What did they talk about? I simply do not believe that you cannot recall what happened here in your club, in your bar, on that morning.'

Albert realised that further obfuscation was no longer an option.

'You seem to have helped refresh my memory with all your questions, officer. Yes. I served them drinks and they went and sat at that table in the corner,' said Albert, pointing to a distant corner of the bar. 'Unfortunately they were too far away for me to hear a word they said.'

Sergeant Sanderson accepted defeat gracefully. 'Yes. No doubt. But how did they appear to you? Were they having a good time? Chatting happily together perhaps. How would you describe their meeting?'

Albert thought about that and decided that he did not have the imaginative powers to convince this rather dour policeman that things at that table had been other than what they were. 'I would describe it as a rather formal meeting ... more in the nature of a business meeting than a social event.'

The sergeant frowned. 'And if you had to make a guess, Mr Hiskins, what would you say was the nature of their business?'

Albert was obviously relieved. 'Ah, there I cannot help you, sergeant. As you see ... they were too far away for me to hear as much as a single word.'

'Yes, I can see that, Mr Hiskins,' said the sergeant. 'But we don't have to hear what people are talking about to get an idea of what might be going on between them, wouldn't you agree? Were they laughing .... were they obviously pleased with each other's company? I'm sure you could tell that even from this distance. I think the experts refer to it as body language. Have you heard that phrase before?'

'I may have now that you come to mention it.'

'And how would you describe it ... their body language?'

'I think I would describe it the same as before ... formal ... as if they were having a business meeting.'

'And you've no idea what the business was about?'

'None at all, sir.'

Sergeant Sanderson decided he had exhausted the possibilities of that conversation.

'Now, I noticed in our visitors' book that Mrs Tracey had also signed in a couple by the name of Connaught. Did she sign them in because she just happened to be on hand when they arrived or were they expected?'

'Oh no sir. The Connaughts were here by arrangement. They all went out for a day on the river on Mr Tracey's boat.'

'The Trident?'

'Yes. A beautiful craft. It's moored at our marina if you want to have a look.'

'Later perhaps. And were you able to gather anything about the relationship between the two groups?'

'Well, from what little I heard I think it is true to say that they had never met before.'

'Really? But the Traceys had invited them out for a day on the river on their boat. A little strange, wouldn't you agree? I mean, there must have been some connection. They couldn't have been complete strangers.'

'No, of course not. I understand that the connection was between Mr Tracey ... Gordon ... and Mr Connaught's father who had died very recently. A rather well-off old gentleman I understand. Mr Gordon used to do odd jobs for him. I think that was the connection. I understand they were very close.'

'And did they have a drink before they set out on the boat?'

'Oh no. The lady was quite definite about. That she didn't think it was a good idea at all.'

'The lady? Mrs Connaught you mean?'

'Yes,'

'And how long were they out on the river would you say?'

Albert thought about that one. 'Three hours, I'd say. Yes, four at most.'

'And when they came back how were they ... chummy? All excited? Pleased, were they? Ready for a drink then perhaps?'

Albert shook his head. 'They never came near the place to my knowledge. Must have got straight in their car and left.'

'A little strange that, wasn't it? I mean, after a pleasant day out surely most people would come in for a drink and relax and talk about what a great time they had.'

Albert nodded eager agreement. 'Yes, but not that pair. They must have gone straight to their car. I certainty didn't see either of them again.'

'And did you form an opinion about the Connaughts. Mrs Connaught in particular.'

'Well the first thing you noticed about Mrs Connaught was that she was wearing altogether too much jewellery for a day on the river. Quite ridiculous in fact.'

'You know she's dead, don't you. Murdered.'

Albert nodded solemnly. 'Yes. I read about it.'

'Did you read about a lot of her jewellery being stolen ... valuable things.'

'Yes, I think I read about that too,' Albert said uncomfortably. He recalled the bitterness in Nola's voice as she commented on that lady's jewellery as she sat with her drink after they returned from the boat. He remembered too the obviously expensive ring that had vanished from Nola's finger the day that loud man with the loud car had come. Then there was Nola's question to Gordon about the key to the house of the old fellow who had died ... presumably Mrs Connaughts late father-in-law.

But he saw no reason to mention any of that to this policeman.

So the policeman's next question was rather a shock. 'I don't suppose you've ever seen any of that missing jewellery, have you, Mr Hiskins.'

The question was asked in such a tone of voice that Albert feared for one moment that this ordinary looking officer of the law had somehow penetrated his thoughts.

He felt his Adam's Apple somersault. 'No. Why should I? Why do you ask?'

'I'm asking the questions, Mr Hiskins. I ask you again; have you ever seen any of Mrs Connaughts jewellery since that day?'

With an effort Albert pulled his thoughts together. 'No. Of course not Why should I? The lady came here only once.'

'And have you discussed these matters with anyone else since then?'

'No, of course not,' said Albert. 'It wouldn't do at all if I started discussing club members business with outsiders.'

'You're the soul of discretion, are you?' asked the sergeant.

Albert was about to issue a defense when he remembered Hodgkiss.

He nodded, head down. 'Actually I did have a conversation with an elderly gentleman who visited here not so long ago.'

'Yes,' said Sanderson. 'I saw his name in the visitors' book, of course. Mr Hodgkiss.'

'Yes. Do you know him?'

'Mr Hiskins ....I said it before: I will ask the questions. But yes, I do know Mr Hodgkiss.'

'Then he can probably tell you more than I about the matter. I found him a rather observant old gentleman .'

'Yes, he is that. So now I will ask you a question for the second time; have you seen any of the jewellery Mrs Connaught was wearing since the day she was here? Think very carefully please, Mr Hiskins.'

It did not take Albert long to convince himself that he could honestly issue a denial, if only on the grounds that Mrs Connaught had been standing too far away for him to clearly see what she was wearing. In spite of that he had a strong feeling, amounting to a certainty, that the emerald ring that had disappeared from Nola's finger during her conversation with that Wisdom fellow had very likely once been the property of that dead lady.

'No. I haven't,' he said with a firm voice that was perhaps a little too loud. But he managed to look the officer squarely in the eye.

Sanderson knew he had no choice but to accept the denial. He pushed back from the bar, put down his half-finished orange juice, and rose. 'I hope nothing happens that leads me to think that you have not been honest with me, Mr Hiskins. Or I'll be back. I may be back anyway,' he said putting a two dollar coin on the bar. Sergeant Sanderson was not a big tipper.

Albert felt very relieved as he watched the sergeant drive away.

*   *   *

Hodgkiss looked up from where he sat in the cramped built-in breakfast nook in the kitchen of the Burke's home.

'Well, Donald,' he asked. 'Anything new to report?'

'I didn't think you'd need to ask me questions like that any more,' said Donald, wriggling his bulk into the narrow seat opposite. 'Doesn't Sanderson tell you all you need to know?'

'No, Donald. Sanderson reports to you ... not me. So what has he been telling you? Anything productive?'

'He visited that club place and wrote a report, but I haven't finished reading it yet. It's about ten pages long but I don't think it's going to tell us much that we don't already know.'

'So what does he say ... the part you've read so far?'

'Just that Wisdom was there recently and had a pow-wow with that Nola Tracey woman ... the one who reckons she was canoodling with her husband in the bush about the same time Mrs Connaught got herself killed.'

'Yes, Donald. I remember who Mrs Tracey is. And this pow-wow Sanderson mentioned. Do we know what was the subject of the pow-wow?'

'No. He said the barman fellah, the only other person in the building at the tine so far as he could tell, said the two of them were sitting too far away for him to hear a word.'

Hodgkiss nodded. 'Surely that in itself suggests something, does it not?'

'It might suggest something to you, Dad, but it doesn't suggest anything much to me. So what do you reckon it was about?'

'It was obviously about something that the two did not want known or they wouldn't have taken steps to ensure that they were not overheard.'

'Oh brilliant. Thanks, Dad. You're always having a go at me for stating the bleeding obvious. Now you're doing it. They didn't want to be overheard … and they weren't. So we're no further ahead, are we?'

'I wouldn't say that at all, Donald. It makes one wonder, does it not, at the relationship between the two. What would they have to talk about that they took such pains for their conversation to remain confidential.'

'Oh that's stretching it a bit, Dad. Perhaps they went to that particular table not because it was away from anywhere they might be overheard, but because it had a nice views of the river, or because it was bigger and more comfortable … anything.'

'Yes, Donald. You may well be right. Now, does Sanderson say whether or not this meeting was pre-arranged? Do we know that?'

'Sanderson said that the Tracey woman signed Wisdom

in in the visitors' book, although that doesn't necessarily mean much.'

'Do you think not, Donald? I do not agree.'

'No. I thought you mightn't.'

'Do we know what time Mr Wisdom arrived?'

'Donald shook his head. 'No. Not exactly. Sanderson said it was in the morning, possibly about mid-morning.'

'Then I would say that very likely this pow-wow was arranged otherwise it is most unlikely that Ms Tracey would have been on hand to meet Wisdom and sign him in. It is not a club with a large membership, Donald, consequently it is not usual for there to be many members present in the morning ... or that was my impression.'

'Yes, I heard about your visit there,' Donald said sourly. 'I suppose you know as much about the place as Sanderson, and about everything that goes on there.'

Hodgkiss ignored the suggestion. 'And what else did Mr Sanderson have to report?'

'He reckoned that the barman, a Mr Hiskins, definitely knew a lot more than he let on.'

Hodgkiss asked. 'About the meeting between Wisdom and Ms Tracey, you mean?'

'Yes. He said the barman reckoned he couldn't hear a word of what they were talking about, but when Sanderson pushed him he said that it didn't appear to be what he would have called a friendly meeting.'

Hodgkiss nodded. 'Well, that tells us something at least. But it would be more helpful to know exactly what was the purpose of the meeting. I cannot imagine for one moment that Ms Tracey, from what little I know of her, would have purposely sought the company of a fellow of Mr Wisdom's stamp.'

'And what, pray, do you think is Mr Wisdom's stamp? I didn't think you knew much about the fellow.'

'Nor do I. But I know enough about to him to realise that he is a ruthless opportunist.'

'And what makes you think that?'

'First there is the way he treats his business associates … and second, it is not usual for the average fair, decent person to find themselves the target of a murderer, wouldn't you agree, Donald?'

'No, Dad. I wouldn't agree at all. That's nonsense. People can get themselves murdered for all sorts of reasons. They can just be in the wrong place at the wrong time. And how many times have you heard reports on the TV of some crim shooting at the wrong house because the person he thought was there had moved out months ago and there was a perfectly innocent family living there. Eh? Tell me that?'

'Yes, Donald, You have a point. But I think a closer examination of the facts will show that Mr Wisdom did not fall into the category of an innocent victim of crime.'

'Possibly not,' Donald conceded. 'So what do you think was going on between them … Wisdom and Mrs Tracey?'

Hodgkiss shrugged. 'I don't know. But I think the time has come when we need to ask the question: *qui bono* … who benefits?'

'OK, Dad. So who do you reckon benefits. I can think of a few.'

'Very well, Donald. So who is at the top of your list of beneficiaries from these two deaths?'

'Well obviously there's Connaught. His wife's death doesn't do him any harm, does it? He won't be exactly mourning her loss, will he? First there's the insurance on all that jewellery and then there was her gambling which, according to reports, was sending him broke.'

'And where did you hear about her gambling?' Hodgkiss asked. 'I was unaware that was common knowledge.'

'It was all there on her phone. During the pandemic many of the TAB shops closed, apparently she used to put on her bets in person, so she just switched to gambling on line. She bet more than ever and in bigger amounts. Much more of it and they'd have been broke. She was addicted, no doubt about that.'

'I agree, Donald. James Connaught won't have been losing any sleep over his loss. But he has an alibi, has he not?'

Donald nodded gloomily. 'Yeah. Now that the doctor's fixed a time of death he's in the clear, or that's what it looks like at the moment.'

'His chess club, you mean?' Hodgkiss asked. 'Have you interviewed the people who were at the club at the time?'

'Yeah. Sergeant Firth went to the club and spoke to some of the players who are regulars there. A couple of then reckoned he'd been there ... that he was there regularly as clockwork every Wednesday. Firth couldn't find anyone who'd actually played against him, but that wasn't unusual. Often they'd play three or four games in one night and it could get a bit confusing about who played who and when. Or that's what Firth said in his report. So if he's right I'd say it's pretty clear that James Connaught was there until after midnight and his wife was dead by 10:30 at the latest. No wriggle room.'

'If it's true then you have a problem there, Donald. But I would double check on Mr Firth's work if I was you. And what about Wisdom. Who stands to gain from that unlovely fellow's demise?'

'Hard to say,' said Donald. 'There's the Bergers who run three of the coffee shops in his chain. Apparently they were behind in their rent and according to the records on Wisdom's phone and emails he'd refused to give then time to pay back rent and they were gone ... kicked out of their three shops after spending years building up the business.'

'A good enough motive,' said Hodgkiss.

'Yeah, except that Angela Bly, Wisdom's manager girl, reckoned that Wisdom'd told her to let them know they could have three months grace to get their act together.'

'And was there any record of that or do you just have the girl's word for it?'

'There was nothing about it on his phone or in his computer, but why would the girl say it if it wasn't true? I can't see that there's anything in it for her. Besides, he'd done similar things for some of the other shop managers who'd got into trouble during the pandemic ... which was about all of them.'

Hodgkiss nodded agreement. 'So there goes the Bergers' motive … provided they knew he was going to let them off before they killed him. Have you spoken to them about where they were at the time Wisdom was murdered?'

'Firth asked them about that. According to them they were at the St James shopping mall all day … or most of it. Saw lots of their friends there.'

'"Saw lots of their friends"' did they. How convenient. They didn't happen to have receipts from any purchases made during the relevant time, did they?'

'Firth never mentioned it. Like I said before … no wriggle room. I'm afraid we're going to have to look somewhere else for our two murderers.'

'Well, Donald, you can look somewhere else if you wish although personally I don't believe they had anything to do with his death. It's too obvious. Too convenient. And the same goes for that Connaught fellow. His wife being killed couldn't have come at a better time to save his bacon. Too damn obvious again. Wouldn't you agree?'

'Yeah. Maybe. But it doesn't alter the facts, does it.'

'Then let's have another look at the facts … see if they are facts … or if there is more to it than people who just happen to have come up with very convenient alibis.'

Donald shook his head. 'Their alibis aren't just convenient Dad. They're watertight. Really watertight.'

'I don't believe there's any such thing as a watertight alibi. In fact the more watertight it is the more suspicious it is. Wouldn't you agree?'

'Maybe, Dad. But not with these two.'

'Perhaps you're right, Donald, but why not look at it from another angle. Haven't you ever read a book or seen a film where two people agree to do a murder for each other. That's what could have happened here. In fact it looks quite likely, don't you agree?'

'No, Dad. I do not agree at all, and I don't intend to waste valuable police resources following up such a crazy idea. It might happen on the movies but I've never heard of it happening in real life. It'd be too obvious anyway. I mean, as you said, it's been done to death on the movies. A fellah'd have to be crazy to think he could get away with it in real life.'

'Very well, Donald. Ignore my advice if you will,' said Hodgkiss wriggling out of the breakfast nook. 'I may look into the matter myself as long as you agree not to accuse me of unwarranted interference in your investigation'

'Go your hardest,' said Donald. 'And good luck. You'll need it.'

Hodgkiss hurried down the hall to his bedroom at the front of the house. Once there he took out his phone, called down a menu and dialed.

'Sergeant Sanderson,' he said. 'Are you busy at the moment.'

In his office at the Crestwood Police Station Sergeant Sanderson replied guardedly. 'That depends.'

'And what might it depend upon?' Hodgkiss asked, knowing what the answer would be.

'It depends on whether or not you have something more

interesting for me to do rather than the meaningless matters I'm wasting my time on at the moment.'

Hodgkiss smiled to himself. 'I think you can safely assume that the small job I have for you will turn out to be more interesting and certainly much more productive than anything the inspector might have allocated to you.'

'Then I'm not busy,' said the sergeant. 'Not busy at all.'

'I'm delighted to hear it, Sergeant. Now, the task I have for you unfortunately will not prove to be a great challenge. In fact you may already have much of the necessary information at your fingertips. It is simply this; would you please ascertain where Mr James Connaught was at the time Mr Wisdom was murdered and where the Bergers were when Mrs Phyllis Connaught met her fate? In order to do this you will need to know the times of death of those two unfortunates ... information that should not be at all difficult for you to come by.'

Sergeant Sanderson smiled to himself. 'I see you subscribe to the superintendent's Collusion Theory.'

'Not necessarily,' said Hodgkiss. 'But it is worth pursuing if only to exclude it.'

Sergeant Sanderson scrambled up from behind his desk. 'Very well. I'll chase them up and arrange times to interview them. They won't be pleased at being asked to produce a second alibi.'

'I'm sure they'll think of something,' said Hodgkiss. 'They've certainly had enough practice.'

It was just on dinner time when Sanderson called back.

'Interesting news, Mr Hodgkiss,' he said. 'Mr Connaught

displayed a wicked lack of imagination. He must be a very devoted chess payer because he was at his club again at the time Mr Wisdom was killed. So I went to the chess club and made a point of speaking to several of the members. Only one of them claimed to have actually played a game against Mr Connaught that day. He said he had played with the white pieces but could not recall which opening he had played against Mr Connaught and could not even recollect the outcome of the game which to me is hardly credible. What do you think?'

'I think the man was obviously lying . covering up.'

'I agree. Then when I pressed him about it he said he thought it had ended in a draw. I found it distressing having to listen to his lies.

'None of the other players were at all sure what time Connaught arrived or left or even if he was actually there at all.'

'Excellent. And the Bergers? Did you find out where they were?'

'Yes. They were at a wedding ...with three hundred other people.'

'Three hundred!' Hodgkiss exclaimed. 'Surely with so many people there they could have slipped away and no one would have noticed.'

'That's what I thought too, Mr Hodgkiss. Trouble is they each did a bible reading during the service.'

'Really? Doesn't that strike you as being just a bit too good to be true?'

'Yes, it does. But they read the lessons all right. Mrs Berger read the first lesson, which was early in the order of service, then returned to her seat which happened to be at the very back of the church. Strangely enough I could find no one who remembered seeing her during the rest of the service or afterwards. The same went for Mr Berger. Everyone remembers him reading the lesson but after that no one is very clear about his whereabouts or his whenabouts. I hasten to add that this is by no means conclusive. They could have both been there. It was not a large church and with a congregation of three hundred it must have been rather full.'

'I understand, sergeant,' said Hodgkiss. 'Now, since Mr Connaught was not playing chess at the time have you had the opportunity yet to ascertain where he was and who he was with?'

'Yes, I approached him and while he was not immediately forthcoming he did eventually provide me with the name and address of a lady with whom he had spent much of the evening in question; a Mrs Jennifer Bright.'

'Well done, sergeant. Now are you going to report to the inspector on your interesting findings.'

There was an awkward silence. 'I would prefer it if you brought the matters to the attention of the inspector, Mr Hodgkiss.'

'Of course. It will be my pleasure, sergeant. But give him your report anyway. It is right that credit is given where it is due. You have done very well … very well indeed.'

'And where do you intend to take the matter from here

Mr Hodgkiss? Any ideas?'

'I have a proposal which could bring the matter to a conclusion ... provided the inspector is prepared to follow it.'

Sergeant Sanderson asked anxiously. 'This proposal ... is it something that is likely to occur to the inspector?'

'Unfortunately not. In fact it is most *unlikely* to occur to him. Why do you ask, sergeant?'

'Then in the interests of harmony is there something I should mention to him ... casually of course. You see, Mr Hodgkiss, I think it would not be in our interests if your proposal brought the case to an end in such a way that none or little of the spotlight fell on the inspector.'

Hodgkiss smiled. 'Yes, Mr Sanderson, I understand. So next time you're talking to the inspector you might remind him that he has a bloody heel print and no matches for it so far. I remember he told me that forensics are of the view that it was very likely a lady's heel print. I think we now have two candidates for a match now, do we not?'

*   *   *

'What on earth did you say to that bloody policeman.'

James Connaught was screaming at his phone ... almost incoherent with rage. 'Two bloody coppers .... one after the other ... asking the same bloody questions.'

Berger was standing in his driveway hosing the family car, phone pressed to an ear, listening in disbelief.

'For Chrissake don't yell at me, James. I thought *you* must have been talking to them. They came here too ... both of them ... wanting to know where I was when your wife disappeared. What the hell was that about? What did you tell them? You know what it looks like, don't you? You were doing your best to put the blame on me for what happened to her.'

'Well you did it, didn't you? You reckoned you did.'

Berger turned off the hose. 'Yes, I know what I said. But I'd just listened to the message you left on my phone. That made it crystal clear that you thought I'd done it. I was confused. I didn't know what to say to you. The fact is I never went near your place that night. I didn't know that anything had happened to your wife until I saw your message and played it. And that's the absolute truth.'

James recalled the rather strange conversation when Berger had finally returned his call.

'Then it wasn't you? Is that what you're saying? You didn't do it ... kill Phyllis ... and you didn't take the jewellery? I thought at the time that you sounded strange ... the way you went on ... not wanting to talk about it. You couldn't get off the phone quickly enough.'

'Yes, and that was because I didn't have a clue what you were on about, except you seemed to think I'd done it ... killed her. And if you believed that then I thought you might get on and keep your half of the bargain and do something about bloody Wisdom. Then when I heard on the radio what had happened to him ... well, naturally I thought you must have done it.'

139

'Well I bloody didn't,' said Connaught. 'I had nothing to do with it.'

'So what did you tell them ... the coppers?'

'The truth,' said Connaught. 'I didn't have a lot of choice, and I can tell you it was bloody embarrassing. I told both of them that I was playing chess when they asked me where I was when Phyl and Wisdom were killed. That's what I always told Phyl when I went out on certain nights. Of course he went to the club and asked around and ... well, I hadn't had a chance to talk to the others to back me up. Actually I was with a friend. And now he'll be off asking her about where I was at the time. Her husband won't be amused if he finds out about us.'

Berger shook his head ruefully. 'None of this would have happened if it hadn't been for my bloody crook knee ... and going to hospital and running into you and your crazy ideas.'

'What are you talking about? None of this had anything to do with us ... these murders. I didn't murder anyone and neither did you, or so you reckon.'

For a moment the conversation stalled as both men thought about what had been said.

'But someone did ... someone murdered them,' said Connaught. 'And whoever did probably has got Phyl's jewellery.'

'Well it wasn't me,' said Berger. 'And come to think of it it's hardly likely that it was the same person killed then both. I can think of one or two people who'd've loved to see Wisdom dead .... other coffee shop operators that he'd treated like shit. But none of them would've known about your wife and her jewellery, because that's probably what it was …. a burglary gone wrong.'

Connaught nodded thoughtfully 'Yeah. You're probably right. Must have been two different people ... two different murderers.'

Berger continued. 'Right. And now I think we really should not have any more to do with each other. I haven't committed any crimes ... the police didn't charge me with anything, so let's get out while the going's good. Agreed.'

'Agreed ... definitely,' said Connaught, cutting the connection.

*   *   *

Inspector Burke had just finished reading a long and detailed report from his sergeant. He put the papers down and looked out of the only window in his office at the brick wall of the adjacent block.

He had no doubt that the report was inspired by his father-in-law because contrary to common sense it established the whereabouts of two of the suspects in his current investigation, but not where they were at the time their obvious murder victims died, but at the time two totally unrelated people had died.

What was the point of finding out where Berger was when Mrs Connaught was killed? There was no connection between the Bergers and the Connaughts that he knew about. And why establish Mr Connaught's whereabouts when Mr Wisdom was killed? Pointless! For the same reason. No connection between the two families.

Just the sort of contrary thing Hodgkiss enjoyed doing.

He pushed back his ancient swivel chair and lumbered down the corridor to Sergeant Sanderson's office.

The sergeant was busy at his desk, slavishly transcribing notes from some interview ... two fingers pecking slowly but accurately at the keyboard of the old black typewriter that he seemed to favour.

The typing continued while Donald stood patiently in the door waiting for his sergeant to acknowledge his presence.

When the sergeant finally paused and looked up, obviously displeased at the interruption, Donald asked. 'Well, what's going on? Anything new?'

Sanderson frowned. Was this the time to mention the bloodstained heel prints as Hodgkiss had suggested? If the inspector had not read his report on the whereabouts or Connaught and Berger he would not see the significance of it. But the inspector had been reading something when he last walked past his office, not looking out the window as usual, so chances are it was the report.

He began. 'I was just thinking about the bloodstained lady's footprint forensics found in Mrs Connaught's bedroom.'

'Yes, what about it, Sergeant?' Donald snapped. 'I hadn't forgotten about it, you know.'

'No, of course not, inspector. It seemed to me that now

we have two ladies who may have ...'

'Yes, I've read your rather strange report on the subject, sergeant. That was my father-in-law's work, was it? The sort of rat-bag idea he'd come up with.'

'I didn't think you'd mind if I ...'

'I don't mind Mr Hodgkiss making suggestions now and then. But I fail to see the relevance of this one.'

'It's just that he thought it may be productive to ascertain the whereabouts of those two ladies when the unrelated deaths occurred. Thinking outside the square I think he would call it.'

Donald nodded. 'No doubt, but 1 know what *I'd* call it. Now, I suppose the next thing he reckons we should do is to get Mrs Berger and Connaught's bit of stuff in and get them to take off their shoes. Is that what Mr Hodgkiss thinks, is it?

'Very likely, although he did not say so to me in as many words.'

'Well, if that's what the Oracle of Lillimoor reckons we should be doing then you'd better get on and do it, hadn't you?'

'Bring them in now, sir?'

'Yes, If it's OK with Dad,' Donald said sarcastically.

Sanderson pulled an old black plastic cover over his typewriter and got up. At the door he paused. 'Do you think the constables downstairs are familiar with the process of taking footprints?'

'God knows,' said Donald. 'If not they'll have to learn fast.

It can't be all that different from taking fingerprints.'

'And another thing, inspector. The ladies concerned may not wish to have their footprints taken. If they refuse should I arrest them and bring them in?'

'Arrest them? Why? What would you charge them with?'

Sanderson shrugged elaborately. 'I had hoped you might give me some guidance there, inspector.' He brightened. 'Perhaps you could come with me and explain it to them.'

Donald shook his head. 'No way, sergeant. Off you go. Do your best. Just say we want them to assist us with our inquiries by excluding some of the forensic evidence from the investigation.'

Sanderson nodded without much enthusiasm. 'I'll give it a try, inspector,' he said heading for the lifts.

The Brights lived in a Macmansion of the very worst kind; huge, decorated in front with four Doric columns and of an overall design that spoke of a total lack of any aesthetic sense.

A young man, shirtless and obviously devoted to physical fitness, was mowing the immaculate lawn in front of the house.

As he watched from his unmarked police car Sergeant Sanderson noticed that the man turned occasionally to look at his home with a smile of proprietorial pride.

The sergeant was about to open the door and step out when he saw an attractive young woman, dressed appropriately for the day, which was hot and sunny, step out onto the front verandah carrying a tray of cool drinks.

Refreshments for her better half, thought the sergeant. Maybe I should wait until she goes back inside so I can have a quiet word with her alone.

But minutes later the mowing was finished, the lawn clippings emptied into a composting barrel beside the garage and the mower stowed in the garage through a side door. Then the couple disappeared, arm in arm, around the side of the house.

Sanderson pushed the car door open and climbed out. He admired the perfection of the lawn as he followed the crazy-paved path to the front door.

When he pressed the button beside the front door an electric bell deep inside the house somewhere played the opening phrases of Beethoven's Ode To Joy.

The young woman, who until then Sanderson had been able to admire only from afar, opened the door.

She smiled. 'Yes?' she asked politely.

'Sorry to interrupt you,' said Sanderson, introducing himself and fishing awkwardly for his identification folder, 'but I wonder if you would mind helping me with an inquiry we have underway at present. You are Jennifer Bright?

The young woman shook her head. 'No. You want my mum.'

For some reason Sanderson felt a surge of relief. 'Do you have an address for your mother?'

'I'd be a pretty poor sort of daughter if I didn't, wouldn't I?' said the young woman, still smiling, but not quite as broadly. 'May I ask why you want to speak to mum?'

Sanderson shook his head. 'I'm sorry, I can't tell you that but no doubt your mother would explain later. I assure you it is nothing for either of you to be concerned about. It is just a question of our investigators being able to exclude certain forensic evidence so they can get on with the job.'

The young woman frowned. 'Forensic evidence? fingerprints, you mean?'

'Exactly,' said Sanderson. Then hastily: 'Or that sort of thing.'

'You want to take my mother's fingerprints?' She was not smiling now.

Sanderson shook his head quickly. 'Oh no. We don't want to take her fingerprints.'

'Then what do you want to do to her?'

'I'm very sorry, but I'm not free to pass on information relating to the investigation. Although I can tell you that it is into two very serious crimes.'

The young woman crossed her arms over an impressive bust. 'Then, much as I take very seriously the public's duty to assist our police, I'm not at all comfortable with putting my mum in a situation that I'm not happy with. Can't you tell me anything more about this investigation, because I can assure you that my mother has not been involved in anything remotely criminal.'

'I don't think for one moment that she has. That is not why I wish to speak with her. The situation is that a man who is involved in the investigation has made a statement that he was in her company at a certain time. I simply need to verify that statement.'

'Are you saying that my mother is some crook's alibi? Is that what you're telling me?' No smiles now.

'I'm sorry, I really cannot comment on that.'

'I'm not asking you to comment. And what about this fingerprint business. If she says she was with this crook then you take her down to the station and fingerprint her. Is that what happens next?'

No flies on this one, Sanderson thought. 'I'm sorry. I can't comment on that either.'

'Then I'm sorry too. But until I know more I can't do anything for you.'

She closed the door firmly.

As he walked back down the path Sanderson heard the girl's voice and another, more mature female voice, in fairly robust discussion. He was tempted to pause and listen but decided to return to the car and try his luck at the next port of call ... the Bergers.

When the Bergers did not answer the bell of their town house Sergeant Sanderson decided to return to the station and report his lack of progress to Inspector Burke.

'Total waste of time then, was it?' the inspector said. It was a statement rather than a question.

'Not entirely,' said the sergeant, loath to admit total failure. 'One thing ... I'd say that Mr Connaught's alibi would stand up if it came to the crunch?'

'Oh. And what makes you say that? You never even spoke to the woman ... this Jennifer Bright ... only her daughter?'

'That's true, but I'd say from her attitude that she knows that her mum's been seeing this Connaught chap and she doesn't approve one little bit. They were having words before I'd got off the front porch.'

'Interesting,' said Donald. 'Well, we won't take mum off the list then. We can try the Bergers tomorrow.'

'We?'

'Yes. Is that all right with you. Are you going to tell Dad about today … about Mrs Bright?'

'Maybe tomorrow. I might have a bit more to report by then.'

*   *   *

Next morning Donald and Sergeant Sanderson were at the Berger's town house shortly before nine o'clock.

Donald made vigourous use of the brass door knocker in the form of an old galleon and when an impatient William Berger finally answered the door he stood fairly across the threshold as if to deny entry.

'What on earth do you people want at this hour,' he said. 'It's not nine yet, and we're just on our way out. Can you come back some other time. Besides, we've already spoken to two policemen including this fellow …' a finger jabbed in Sanderson's direction … 'so I can't imagine what other questions you could possibly have.'

'Actually we don't have any more questions,' said Donald.

'Then what on earth *do* you want?'

'It's Mrs Berger I would like to see. Is she at home?'

'Yes, but she's busy right now.'

'Busy?'

'Yes, officer. She works from home.'

'She runs coffee shops from home?'

'Running three coffee shops involves much more than pouring coffee and putting croissants on plates. There is stock to be ordered, there are wages to be paid, invoices to be check and paid ... no end of things to be done that can very conveniently be done from home.'

'No doubt' said Donald, unabashed. 'Nevertheless we need to see your wife as a matter of urgency.'

'So it's urgent now, is it? So why's it so urgent today when it wasn't urgent the other day when other fellows came asking questions?'

Donald explained in his most reasonable voice. 'We have forensic material that needs to be checked in order to exclude certain parties from our inquiries.'

'Certain parties ... my wife you mean?'

Donald nodded. 'Yes, It would be very helpful if we could exclude her from our inquiries at this point. To save time.'

'And what would she have to do in order to be "excluded from your inquiries", if it's not a rude question?'

'It's very simple. We just want to see her feet,' said Donald.

Berger's jaw dropped. 'See her feet?! You can't be serious?'

Donald drew himself up. 'Mr Berger, Sargent Sanderson and I are conducting an investigation into two murders, including the murder of your former employer ...'

Berger cut him off. 'That man was not my employer, officer. Please understand that.'

'Very well, licensee or whatever he was. The point is he is dead … murdered … and in circumstances where you had a lot to lose if he was still alive and kicking. Right?'

'Perhaps. But what on earth has this got to do with my wife's feet?'

Donald shook his head. 'I'm not in a position to go into those sort of details with you, Mr Berger. And if your wife chooses not to cooperate then I will have no choice but to take her down to the station for questioning on a variety of matters.'

'But she's already been questioned … twice. What more do you want to ask her?'

'There are aspects of her statement about her presence at the church service you were attending that are far from satisfactory.'

Berger shook his head in bewilderment. 'You can't be serious. But she read the lesson. Hundreds of people saw her …. heard her.'

'Yes. Yes, she read the lesson, the first lesson, then she went to sit at the back of the church where she could have slipped out then returned later unnoticed. Now, if she would just show us her feet then perhaps …'

Berger flung up his hands. 'OK. OK. Just wait here. I'll go and get her.'

At the foot of the stairs he stopped and turned. 'I suppose you'd better go in there,' he said indicting a sitting room to the left off the hall. 'We don't want my wife having to strip off on the front verandah.' Then. 'Your superiors are going to hear about this.'

Donald and the sergeant were crowded together uncomfortably on a very small two-seater lounge covered in a floral tapestry when Mrs Berger appeared at the door. She was not happy. 'What's this nonsense about you wanting to see my feet?'

'It's just a formality, Mrs Berger,' said Donald with an attempt at charm. 'We wish to exclude you from our inquiries. That's all.'

'And how is looking at my feet going to exclude me from your inquiries ... whatever they're about? There's nothing unusual about my feet.'

'I'm sure there's not and that will mean we won't have to bother you again.'

'Good,' she said with feeling as she sat down heavily on a small pouf decorated with petty-point roses. She looked up at Donald. 'Which foot do you want?'

Donald turned to Sanderson with a raised eyebrow.

'The right, I think it was,' said Sanderson in a stage whisper.

Mrs Berger had heard. She pulled off a brown slip-on shoe with a very low heel and a white sock. She thrust her bare right foot up towards Donald.

Donald examined the foot, clearly disappointed. 'Now the other foot if you please, Mrs Berger.'

'Why? What's wrong with that one?' she asked, disappointed.

'Its not the one we're looking for?'

'How do you know? You hardly looked at it.'

'The one we're looking for doesn't have a scar on the heel like yours.'

Mrs Berger began replacing the sock and shoe. 'I thought that must have been it. I got that swimming when I was a little girl. It was a broken bottle or a shell or something in the surf. I was only five at the time and it bled like mad. My mother had conniptions. She thought I was going to die of blood poisoning or something. She took me straight to the doctor who gave me an anti-tetanus injection.'

By the time Mrs Berger had finished relating the history of her scar she had removed her left shoe and sock.

She raised the foot for inspection. 'How's this one. Do I get excluded from you inquires now?'

Donald glanced at the foot and shook his head, trying unsuccessfully to hide his disappointment. 'That's fine, he said. 'Sorry to have bothered you, Mrs Berger.'

As he accompanied them to the front door Mr Berger asked: 'And do you intend to keep hounding our friends from the church trying to make them swear that my wife wasn't there?'

'We were not hounding anyone, Mr Berger. We are conducting a murder investigation. It is a very serious matter.'

Berger asked. 'And are you any near to finding who killed her?'

Donald stopped abruptly mid-stride and turned. '"Her", Mr Berger? Who are you referring to?'

'Why, whoever you're investigating or course,' Berger stumbled.

'But you said "her". Why do you think it's a woman we're investigating?'

'I didn't say it was a woman,' said Berger with unlikely emphasis.

'You did, Mr Berger. We both heard you,' Donald said turning to Sanderson who nodded enthusiastic agreement.

'Then you must have heard wrong. I said no such thing,' said Berger retreating to the safety of his verandah. 'And I will be reporting this blatant harassment to your superior officers.'

He slammed the door.

'Well that right heel print … it certainly wasn't hers, was it,' said Donald gloomily. 'If forensics are right and it was a woman's then we've run out of feet to compare it with.' He brightened. 'Hey, you don't think there are some children mixed up in this business that we haven't come across yet?'

Sanderson shook his head. 'Not that I've noticed so far, sir. Will I bring Mr Hodgkiss up to date and ask him about the children.'

Donald nodded. 'Yeah, bring him up to date, but don't mention the children. He'd never let me forget it.'

As soon as they arrived back at the station Sergeant Sanderson went to his office, took out his phone, found a number and dialed.

'Yes, Sergeant Sanderson,' came a familiar voice. 'And how did this morning's exercise turn out?'

'Much as you expected, Mr Hodgkiss. We drew blanks

on both visits. The daughter of the first lady would not allow access to her mother although I have reason to believe that if Mr Connaught's alibi was ever tested in court he would come through with flying colours. I say this because as I was leaving the premises I heard the beginning of an acrimonious conversation between the daughter and an older woman with a distinctly north-of-England accent, a lady who I have courageously assumed to be Connaught's mistress.'

'A reasonable assumption, sergeant,' said Hodgkiss. 'So the visit was not entirely wasted. Connaught was very likely telling the truth.'

'I agree. The second lady in question, Mrs Berger, eventually presented her feet for inspection after her husband had attempted to run interference for her. The heel of interest, her right heel, had a large scar across it, ruling it out immediately. And the other heel the inspector dismissed at a glance. I assume he had a clear idea in his mind of what to look for.'

'A very rash assumption this time, sergeant. One never quite knows that is in the sergeant's mind from one day to the next.'

'So what now, Mr Hodgkiss. We appear to have exhausted the supply of ladies with feet to examine. You don't think perhaps a child might be involved, do you?'

'Hardly. Is that what Donald thinks?' Hodgkiss asked, with a chuckle. 'I wouldn't be surprised.'

'Oh no,' said the sergeant. 'It was entirely my idea. Entirely.'

'I hope your loyalty does not go unrewarded, sergeant,' said Hodgkiss. 'However, I must disagree if you think we have exhausted the supply of ladies with feet worth examining. You appear to have forgotten one very memorable lady ... that sea-dog Ms Nola Tracey.'

'I hadn't forgotten that lady,' said the sergeant. 'I just have not had the pleasure of her acquaintance.'

'Then it's high time we remedied that omission, what do you say?'

'I think it is more a question of what the inspector might say,' said the sergeant. 'I don't think I could make another trip to the cruising club without his knowledge and approval.'

'I'm not suggestion you should. This time I think we should all go ... the three of us. Besides it is a very pleasant drive and the club itself, while not lavishly appointed, is nevertheless comfortable and I found Albert, the barman, to be most obliging with information although he is not always aware of it. Now, will you raise the question of the visit with Donald or would you prefer that it did it?'

'I think you would put the question of the trip beyond doubt, Mr Hodgkiss.'

'Very well, sergeant. I will ring him now and no doubt he will inform you of the arrangements.'

* * *

Next morning, when Hodgkiss rang on the private line to his office, Donald decided to be difficult.

'Nola Tracey,' he said. 'Never heard of the lady.' The moment the words had left his mouth Donald knew he would regret them.

Hodgkiss was quick to take advantage of the lapse. 'Then I must conclude that you have not been paying proper attention to your job, Donald. Mrs Tracey and her husband, Gordon, are mentioned frequently in Sergeant Sanderson's detailed records of interviews which must have crossed your desk.'

'Oh yes. I know all about that,' said Donald, determined to extricate himself from the situation without loss of face. 'But what makes you think that this Nola Tracey might be a person of interest.'

Hodgkiss held his breath and counted slowly to ten.

'Hello. Are you still there, Dad?'

'Yes, and I'm starting to wonder why. Either you're interested in pursuing this investigation in a sensible fashion or you are not. If not please say so now and I will make other arrangements.'

'But I just can't understand why you think she's got anything to do with those two murders.'

'Can't you? Really? Well, for a start she knew both the Connaughts. Nola Tracey and her husband took the Connaughts out on their boat shortly before Mrs Connaught was killed. It was not a happy day on the water. We know they were not friends. That, and the fact that her husband's car registration number was on Wisdom's phone require explanation. Don't you think that's enough to make it worthwhile taking an interest in the lady?'

'No, Dad. Not really. But if you reckon we should have a talk to her, OK, we'll take a run out there. Where is this Cruising Club place?'

'Mr Sanderson knows the way. Let him drive us there.'

'And since when do you arrange my staff's work roster. Besides, why take Sanderson along. What use is he going to be?'

'Really, Donald, I'm surprised you ask. Sergeant Sanderson is familiar with all the details of both cases and he knows how to find the club which is in a rather remote location. Two excellent reasons.'

'You two are getting pretty chummy aren't you? I can't say that I'm all together happy about that.'

'Really, Donald. And do you have any complaints about how Sanderson has been performing during this rather complex investigation? Has he kept you fully informed of all developments; has he ignored significant evidence; has he failed to gather important information during interviews. I think his observations about Mrs Bright's mother were quite insightful. One wonders whether you would have been up to the task in the circumstances.'

'OK OK, Dad. Enough. Anything else.'

'Yes. I think it may be wise to have the scene-of- crime team follow us to the club and have a close look at the Tracey's boat.'

'You don't think she killed Mrs Connaught on the boat, surely?'

'No, Donald, that is a ridiculous idea. I suggest the forensic team look at the boat simply because the Connaughts spent about four hours on board and they may find DNA evidence that could be useful.'

'OK. Fair enough. We'll start first thing in the morning. You fix it with Sanderson. Right?'

* * *

Nola Tracey, dressed in cut-down denim shorts, her trademark midriff top, and neat white sand shoes, looked up from the section of brass rail she had been polishing.

A dark sedan had just stopped in the club's car park. The two passengers' side doors opened and an elderly man with a short well-trimmed beard climbed out of the rear compartment.

Nola decided this would be the fellow Hodgkiss who Albert had described to her.

The man who got out of the front compartment had copper written all over him; tall, hefty and carried himself with something of a swagger.

The man who climbed out of the driver's seat also was a copper, built on smaller, finer lines, but unmistakable nevertheless.

Nola said quietly. 'They're here.'

Gordon, who was below decks working on the Trident's

engine, heard her. 'Who's here?' he called back, not too loud.

'The coppers. Just pulled up in the car park. Two coppers and the old guy Albert told us about ... he was here asking questions. You remember.'

'How do you know it's them?'

'Come and have a look. Do you have your phone there. We're going to need it.'

'It's in my pocket.'

'Good . Then come on up and say hello ... pleasantly.'

Gordon scrambled up the narrow companionway ... shorts, shirtless and bare feet. He glanced towards the car park. 'I see what you mean. The skinny one ... that'll be Sanderson,' he said, wiping grease from his hands on a rag he had brought up with him from below.

'Why do you think they're here,' he asked standing beside his wife. 'What do they want?'

Nola shook her head. 'I've no idea, but it might be to do with my feet because that's where they're looking ... the three of them ... wondering why I'm not barefoot, I suppose. The Connaught woman must have said something to someone about having to take her shoes off on board before she got herself murdered. Something else she had to complain about. God she was awful.'

Nola and Gordon stood silently, side by side on the deck watching the group of men approaching.

The one with the beard raised a hand in greeting. 'Mr and Mrs Tracey, is it?'

'That's Hodgkiss,' Nola said quietly. 'Albert said he's sharp as a tack but could be on our side once he's got the full story.'

'Then let's hope Albert's right … though he usually is with people.'

Gordon called in reply. 'That's us. And who might you be?'

Hodgkiss kept walking while the two behind him stopped. 'Hodgkiss … Edgar Hodgkiss.'

'And your friends?' Gordon asked.

'The larger of the two is my son-in-law, Detective Inspector Donald Burke and the other is Sergeant Sanderson.'

Gordon turned to his wife. 'Officers of the law, darling,' he said in a voice that carried. 'I think you mentioned something about the police calling, didn't you?'

Nola nodded. 'So I did. But I'd almost given up. I thought they'd've called before now. I hope they weren't waiting for an invitation.'

Donald stepped forward. 'Well, we're here now, Mrs Tracey. Obviously you know *why* we're here so let's stop playing games.'

Hodgkiss stepped forward. 'God, woman, what happened to your face … and your arms … the bruising.'

'Good of you to notice,' said Nola, raising a hand to a sticking plaster on her left cheek. The hand moved on to touch another plaster covering a wound on the side of her neck. 'I'll give you the full story inside,' she said tossing her head in the direction of the club house.

She climbed down from the deck to the marina in one

fluid, graceful movement. 'My husband will sign you in … rules you know.'

The three men followed Nola with interest. In the entry foyer she stopped and pointed to the counter against the far wall. 'The Visitors' book is over there. I'll see you in the bar.'

The three signed their names and Gordon added his in the next column. 'Let's get this over with,' he said, and led the way through to the bar where Albert was setting a gin and tonic down in front of Nola who was perched prettily on a high stool.

She turned with a smile. 'And what will be your pleasure gentlemen?' she asked. 'The drinks are on us"

'I don't think so, Mrs Tracey,' said Donald. ' I won't be drinking nor will the sergeant unless he'd like something soft. Mr Hodgkiss can drink what he likes but I'd rather he paid for his own.'

Nola took the rebuff gracefully. 'As you wish, inspector.'

'Make mine a red wine, please, Mrs Tracey' said Hodgkiss, 'and a mineral water for the sergeant. I'll pay for both to avoid silly complications.'

Nola nodded to Albert who started preparing the drinks. She turned to Donald. 'Very well, Inspector Burke. Here we all are … at last. How may we help you.'

Before Donald could get a word out Hodgkiss said: 'Inspector Burke has a foot fetish. He wants to look at your feet.'

Nola raised an eyebrow. 'I've heard about people like that.'

161

She turned to Donald. 'Do you have a preference for feet ... left or right?'

'Right,' said Donald, not amused.

'Right it is,' said Nola. She leaned down to remove the sand shoe, at the same time offering the men an interesting view down her loose top.

When the sand shoe was off Nola raised the sole for Donald's inspection.

Donald and Sanderson both gaped at the foot in horror. Hodgkiss chuckled.

Sanderson asked, not without sympathy, 'whatever happened to your foot, Mrs Tracey? That looks very painful.'

Nola looked up, smiling, grateful for the attention. 'It *was* rather painful at first, but it's healing up quite nicely now, thank you.'

Donald stepped forward, his face stony. 'Mrs Tracey can you please explain what you have done to your foot ... and why?'

'Of course, inspector. It's quite simple really. For years my husband and I have gone everywhere barefoot. It's become our way of life. Ask anyone in the club. We hardly ever wear anything on our feet, except to official club functions of course, then every one comments ... makes jokes. Consequently our feet became very tough over the years. Well, recently we decided that this had made our feet look pretty awful; calloused and really ugly. They were not a pretty sight, believe me.'

'They're not a very pretty sight now,' said Sanderson, 'if your left foot looks anything like your right.'

'I'm afraid it does,' said Nola. 'It had the same treatment.'

Hodgkiss asked. 'How did you achieve such an appalling outcome?'

Gordon said. 'Pumice stone and plenty of elbow grease. I did Nola's and she did mine.'

Donald growled. 'It's not going to save you ... doing that.'

'Save us,' Nola echoed, innocence itself. 'Save us from what?'

'You know "from what" ... from charges of murdering Phyllis Connaught and Mr Wisdom.'

Nola came quickly to her feet. 'I have murdered no one, inspector. No one.'

Donald shook his head. 'That's for a jury to decide, Mrs Tracey. Not me.'

'So are you going to charge me? Is that why you came here today?'

'Not altogether,' said Donald. 'Mostly I came here because Mr Hodgkiss insisted it would be worth the visit, and it looks like he might be right ... this time.'

'Because of my feet, you mean? What do you think they prove?'

'They prove you were there at the time ... at Mrs Connaughts home ... and they prove that you knew you'd left a bloody footprint behind after you'd attacked her. Obviously that's why you decided to scrub your footprints off. You thought if you got rid of them we couldn't prove you were there.'

Hodgkiss held up a hand. 'Hold it there, Donald. What

you said is right … mostly. But it's not the point … not the point at all. The scoured soles are certainly proof of something, but it's something altogether different.'

'What do you mean … "something altogether different?" What are you trying to say?'

'I'm saying that Mrs Tracey did not know at the time that she'd left a footprint behind. That is an important fact and you should have realised that as soon as you saw Mrs Tracey's feet.'

'Oh and why should I have realised that?'

'Because obviously Mrs Tracey would not have left the footprint behind had she known it was there. She would have taken it away which would have been a simple matter seeing it was on a small piece of tissue paper. But since the forensic officer found it under the bed it was unlikely she would have noticed it in the drama of the moment.

'But she knew nothing about it at the time … she couldn't have.'

Donald shook his head. 'No, Dad. She must have known about it at the time because we were very careful not to mention it in the information we gave out to the press.'

'Then your forensic officer or one of the other scene-of-crime officers must have told someone.'

Donald bristled. 'No way. Our scientific people don't blab about their work … not about important details like that … facts that have to be kept from he public.'

He hesitated and raised a hand. 'But wait on … there is someone else who new about it. Connaught. He knew about it. He was there when it was found. The forensics fellow commented on it ... gave a bit of lecture about it.'

Hodgkiss shook his head. 'No, Donald. I don't believe Connaught would've told her.' He turned to Nola. 'It wasn't Connaught that told you about the bloody heel print, was it?'

'No, it wasn't. But I'd like to know why you're so sure it wasn't him?'

'It couldn't have been Connaught,' said Hodgkiss. 'If he was there when the forensic officer found it he would have known all about it ... whether it was the left foot, right foot, toes, heel ... the lot. But whoever told you about it had no idea of the details.'

Nola nodded. 'You're right about that. All I was told was that there was a bloody footprint found in the Connaught's bedroom. I knew it had to be mine because I'd gone in barefoot for obvious reasons, and later I noticed I'd cut my foot on something, probably while Mrs Connaught was trying to throttle me or tear my hair out by the roots.'

Hodgkiss continued. 'And if you'd known which foot made the print, and that it was the heel only, you wouldn't have damaged both your feet in this quite barbaric and unnecessary manner. You would have treated just the heel of the right foot. Right? Oh, and another thing. When your skin grows back as it soon will, so will the prints ... exactly the same as before.'

Nola was aghast. 'You're joking.'

Hodgkiss shook his head. 'Fingerprints and footprints are formed during the first three months of gestation. They are yours for life … no matter how you try to remove them.'

Sergeant Sanderson, determined to keep the investigation on course, asked: 'So who *did* tell you about the bloody footprint?'

Nola turned to Gordon. 'Does it matter if we tell them?'

Gordon shrugged. 'I don't see why. She didn't swear you to secrecy, did she?'

Nola turned again to face Donald. 'It was Wisdom's girlfriend.'

'Which one?' Sanderson asked. 'He had a few, I understand.'

'The one who worked for him. Angela. She told me about it. That's all she knew. A bloody footprint was found in Mrs Connaught's bedroom. I asked if she knew any details, but she didn't, or she said she didn't. And in case you're wondering, I've no idea who told her about it.'

'I don't see that it matters who told her?' said Donald.

'Do you not?' Hodgkiss demanded angrily. 'Then I can only say that it is typical of your slap-dash approach to investigation. We are told a crucial piece of information and you aren't interested in pursuing it further. Someone has disclosed details from a crime scene and you don't want to know who did it or why … and worst of all it appears you don't care,'

Donald seethed. 'We'll get back to Wisdom's secretary later … don't worry about that.'

'But I do worry, Donald. By the time you get around to it that lady will have invented some story to explain her knowledge, if she feels the need.'

'I'll cross that bridge when I come to it,' said Donald. 'But right now I want to hear from this lady ...' a finger jabbed at Nola. 'You reckon you didn't murder anyone. OK then. Tell us ... what were you doing at Mrs Connaught's place that night. What happened? What did you do with the jewellery. Why did you remove her from the scene? Everything.'

Nola settled back on the stool. 'All right inspector. Everything. I suppose you could say it started right here in this bar ... on the morning we took the two of them out in the boat.

'Of course we both knew in advance that it would very likely turn out to be a complete disaster ... and it did.

'You see the whole purpose of the day out was to touch James Connaught for a large sum of money because we were broke. And we were broke mainly due to bad share advice from James' father ... a gentleman known as Old Mick who, incidentally had died the previous week leaving James a very wealthy man.

'For years Gordon had been doing odd jobs for old Mick ... plumbing, carpentry, gardening ... everything. And Old Mick used him up mercilessly and paid him nothing ... in money. Yes, he took Gordon and sometimes both of us out for very nice meals at some pretty flash restaurants, and he often gave Gordon tips on the share market ... usually very good tips and there's no doubt that we made a lot of money from them over the years. We're not denying that.

'But with the latest tip ... well it turned into a disaster because without telling me Gordon went out and borrowed money so he could really go in hard. The share flopped and we were left seriously broke. We hoped that James would come to our rescue since it was on his father's say-so that we bought the shares.

'But of course it never happened. James reckoned that he'd lost heavily on the shares and his wife .... well she was raising objections at every point.

'But I could have handled that ... her telling us how we were greedy and deserved everything we got ... if it hadn't been for the jewellery. She turned up here to go out on the boat as if she was going to a royal garden party. She was absolutely dripping diamonds and pearls and rubies. You name it, she was wearing it. And I knew that she'd done it deliberately to show me up.

'That was when I decided that I was going to take all that stuff away from her. I knew that Gordon had a key to the big house where Old Mick lived and of course James and the awful Phyllis had already moved in there before the old guy was cold. Couldn't wait to get in and play lord of the manor. So we didn't even have to break in. If James had thought about it he'd probably have realised that Gordon must have had a key to the place since he sometimes did work there when Old Mick was away overseas somewhere.'

'Enough of the history, Mrs Tracey,' Donald snapped. 'What happened the night you went there?'

Hodgkiss held up a hand. 'Not so fast, Donald. I think Mrs Tracey would be wise to have her solicitor present?'

Nola held up a hand. 'No solicitors. I know what I did was wrong and I'm prepared to take my medicine. But I did not murder that woman. It could easily have turned out the other way round.

'And another thing ... Gordon didn't want any part of it. He came along only to make sure I didn't do anything I shouldn't ... other than taking the jewellery of course, though he wasn't really in favour of that either.'

'I'll make a note of it,' said Donald, stony faced.

'Please do,' said Nola. 'Now, when we got there it must have been around ten or perhaps a bit later. The house was quite dark ... no light on anywhere. We knew James was out playing chess somewhere, or he was supposed to be, and we thought we'd just get in and out again in no time at all. Of course Gordon knew the whole house inside out and back to front. He gave me the key. We went in. Up the stairs to the main bedroom. No lights needed because there was plenty of moonlight. And we both had our shoes off as usual. I was just going through the drawers in this big chest just to the left of the bedroom door when she woke up and turned on a bedside lamp.

'It gave enough light to see us and she recognised us straight away. She literally jumped out of bed and ran straight at me swearing and yelling what she was going to do. She was a big strong woman and I doubt if I could have held on to her for much longer. You can see what she did to me. She scratched my face, my neck, she tried to choke me. Look at my arms. The bruises have faded now but you should have seen them the next day. Black and blue I was and I have the photos to prove it.

'I know you people look under the fingernails of murder victims to see if you can find samples of the skin of the killer . Well, have a look under *her* fingernails and you'll find quite a lot of my skin there. And you can see where it came from.

'Anyway, Gordon had to come to the rescue or I would have been dead meat in another minute. He dragged her off me although she was still shouting and screaming and scratching.

'Then all of a sudden she just went quiet and collapsed on the carpet.

'I thought she was dead … that she'd had some sort of seizure.'

'What about the blood?' Donald demanded 'There was blood all over her. One of you, you or your husband, must have hit her … roughed her up.'

Gordon shook his head. 'No way. I didn't hit her. I took hold of her in a headlock and tried to drag her off Nola.'

'Then how do you account for the blood all over her?'

'I guarantee when your people come to test it they'll find it was my blood all over her,' said Nola. 'Or most of it was.'

Donald nodded. 'OK. No point going into that now. So she collapsed all of a sudden. What did you do then?'

'I thought she was dead … we both did … that she'd had a heart attack or something like that. All I wanted to do then was to get out of there … take her away , leave her somewhere and get home and think about what we should do.'

Sergeant Sanderson asked: 'But why did you remove the body? Why not just leave her there?'

Nola shook her head helplessly. 'I'm sorry, sergeant. I simply have no answer for you. But you're right. With hindsight we should have just cleared out and left her there, but somehow it just didn't seem right, leaving her there like that. We thought we should take her somewhere not too far away, leave her and ring the police or ambulance to come and get her ASAP.

'So we put here in her own car, the keys were by the bed, I drove to the national park with Gordon following in our car. We left her at a little spot we knew from our courting days. On the way home we saw a public phone box and Gordon rang the police and said exactly where she was.

'We put some leaves and twigs and things over her to cover her up a bit,' said Gordon. 'We didn't like to leave her just lying there in her nightie.'

Donald muttered. 'How very thoughtful of you.'

'We're not proud of what we did,' said Nola. 'I must have been out of my mind.' She turned to Gordon. 'And I shouldn't have involved you in the whole awful business.'

'It's a good job you did,' said Gordon. 'That woman could have killed you.'

Nola asked. 'Now, Inspector Burke. Where do we go from here?'

'You'll both have to come to the station and make a

statement about what happened, then you'll be charged with burglary, assault and with offenses relating to moving the body.'

'I still have the jewellery …. except for a ring. And I know where that is. James can have all of it back.'

Hodgkiss asked. 'So you both believed she was dead when you left her there?'

Nola looked at Gordon. 'I certainly did.'

Gordon nodded.

'Did either of you do anything to ascertain whether or not she really was dead? I mean did you feel her pulse … anything like that?'

The two looked at each other then shook their heads.

Hodgkiss continued. 'You say Mrs Connaught attacked you as soon as she woke up?'

'Yes. She just opened her eyes, saw me there, jumped out of bed and flew at me. And she knew it was me because she shouted my name.'

'Perhaps you did something to wake her. Did you knock something over? Did either of you cough … make a noise?'

'No. Nothing like that. She just woke up.'

'And during this fracas … you say she tried to strangle you and that she scratched you on the face and the throat … what damage did you inflict on her?'

Nola shook her head. 'I doubt if I inflicted any damage on her … not that I'm aware of. I was too busy protecting myself, and I didn't make much of a job of that … as you see,' she said touching the plaster on her throat again.

Sanderson asked 'Then you'll be surprised to learn that she received a heavy blow to the back of the head?'

Nola's surprise was evident. 'Surprised! I'd be amazed. And relieved, because now I *know* I had nothing to do with her dying. No way did I ever hit her on the back of the head … heavily or even softly. In fact I doubt if I actually hit her at all … anywhere. I was grappling with her, trying to control her. Yes. That's the best way to describe it … I was grappling with her. It seemed like forever but I suppose it was really only a minute or two … if that.'

'OK,' said Donald, his disappointment evident. 'Now we know what happened to her … to Mrs Connaught. Now, let's come to Mr Wisdom. What have you got to say about him. You reckon you didn't kill him either, I suppose?'

'Certainly not,' said Nola. 'I was there when he died. I won't deny that. But if you want to know what happened … everything that happened … I can show you … in detail and in colour, although I assure you it will give me no pleasure.'

'Show us?' Donald demanded skeptically. 'How will you show us? Did you video everything.'

'No. I didn't. He did.'

'Wisdom, you mean?' Donald asked. 'Why? Why would he do that?'

'To show to his friends later and put it on the internet. That's what he told me. Apparently he did it with a lot of the women who went there with him. Now come and I'll show you. Through here. I've got it all set up.'

Nola led the way out of the bar, across the entry lobby and

into a small room dominated by a huge television screen. A number of wooden chairs were set around the screen in a semicircle.

'Don't get too comfortable because this won't take long,' she said.

'But before I start let me give you a bit of the background to how this happened. Two days ago I had a call from Mr Wisdom out of the blue. I didn't know him although I knew he owned a string of coffee shops and because I was a regular customer at one of them, the one at St James. I'd seen him coming and going there on occasions.

'When he rang he said he wanted to see me. He had something I'd be very interested in and would I meet him in the car park near his coffee shop at St James. Naturally I was pretty curious about what he wanted to show me, so I agreed to met him. When we met he took me to his car and he showed me some photos of Gordon and I dumping Mrs Connaught in the bush.

'At first I denied that it was us. I said the pictures were so poor it could have been anyone, although of course you could see it was Gordon and I.

'Anyway, he called my bluff. He said if I was so sure it wasn't us in the pictures we wouldn't mind if he took them straight to the police. Of course I didn't want that and since I thought he was just trying to shake us down for some money I asked him how much he wanted for the pictures. He said he didn't want anything ... not money. He said he'd seen me around the shopping centre and he really fancied me. He said I could have the photos if I'd sleep with him. I decided that would probably be no worse than having the police on our doorstep asking questions about the Connaught woman and her jewellery so I agreed and we fixed a time for me to go to his unit.

'As soon as I arrived he wanted to take me straight to the bedroom, but I told him that nothing like that was going to happen until he'd given me the photos.

'To my surprise he agreed. He went to a drawer in one of the bedside tables and took them out, four of them, and handed them to me. I took them straight to the ensuite, ripped them into little pieces and flushed them down the toilet.

'After that I kept my part of the bargain, as you'll see. But he didn't, which is hardly surprising, knowing the man.

'When we'd finished having sex I was just about to start getting dressed when he told me he wanted to do it again. I told him no … that we'd made a deal and I'd kept my part of it. Then he told me that he had more photos and that he'd send then to the police if I refused.

'I was so mad I told him he could send them and that I was leaving. That's when things started to get out of hand. He said if I didn't do certain things he wanted, things I'd only do with Gordon, he'd rape me and enjoy doing it.

'Anyway, I tried to get dressed but he grabbed me and started to drag me back to the bed. I was in no doubt that he was going to rape me. So when he pushed me over onto the bed I drew my legs up, planted my feet on his chest and just kick him away. It's all there on the video.

'Anyway, as you'll see, I kicked him maybe harder than I should have, but I really was terrified of what he might do to me. How often do you hear of men raping women then killing them to stop them telling. That's what I thought was going to happen to me.

'Anyway, after I'd kicked him away he lost his balance and staggered across the room backwards and fell, hitting his head on the base of that marble washstand near the door to the ensuite. He just lay there. I never thought at the time that he might have been seriously hurt. I thought he was just knocked out ... unconscious.

'I got dressed and I had a look at him and he seemed fine. He was breathing OK, although he was still unconscious. His head had been bleeding a bit but there were no great pools of blood.

'I thought maybe I'd ring an ambulance after I'd left and suggest they go to the address and check him out. I left the door ajar so they could get in.

'But before I left I thought I should have a look around for these other photos he said he had. I found them in the same drawer of his bedside table as the ones he'd given me earlier, and I took the away with me.

'But I'm positive he was breathing when I left, so he was definitely alive then.

'Now I'll show you what actually happened so you can all see for yourselves that what I've said just now is the honest truth,' she said, operating a TV remote control.

The big screen came to life. It showed part of the interior

of a large expensively furnished bedroom. A huge bed was in the middle of the picture.

Nola commented. 'The master bedroom at Wisdom's unit. As you see, he had the camera trained on the bed. He must have made lots of videos there with God knows how many poor girls.'

Then from the right of the screen Wisdom came into view. He was stark naked. He was leading a naked Nola by the hand.

'Do you mind if I fast forward here?' Nola asked.

When no one objected the figures went into such rapid motion that their frantic coupling on the bed appeared more comic than erotic.

Hodgkiss noticed that neither Donald nor Sergeant Sanderson appeared to be enjoying what was happening on the screen.

Donald was watching with a frantic scowl and the sergeant's head was turned away but his eyes were dutifully paying attention to the screen.

Then Donald interjected. 'Hold it there, please. I want to see what happens now.'

At this point Nola had risen from the bed and was walking towards the side of the screen from which she and Wisdom had appeared.

Nola froze the picture. 'What happens now is the part I particularly want you to see,' she said.

Although there was no sound it appeared that Wisdom, still laying on the bed, had called Nola back. She stopped on the edge of the picture and turned, apparently listening to something Wisdom was saying. His mouth was moving quickly and he was pointing towards Nola's hand.

Nola dropped the hand to her side then moved it behind her back.

'He wanted me to give him my ring?' she explained. 'I should have taken it off before I got there.'

'You say it's your ring?' Donald queried. 'I'd say it's more likely one of the pieces you stole from Mrs Connaught. Right?'

Nola froze the picture 'Yes, of course it was. I could never have afforded something like that. And he knew it was hers because he saw me take it off her hand.'

'When you and your husband took her out to bury her?'

Nola nodded. 'Yes. Now look what happens next.' She operated the remote and the figures began to move again.

Wisdom rolled quickly across the bed and with one hand seized Nola by the wrist and with the other wrenched the ring from her finger. He placed the ring on the bedside table without releasing the wrist then with a single powerful jerk pulled Nola back onto the bed.

Nola said. 'He demanded to have sex again and I told him no. Then he said that was too bad because he was going to anyway, and if I didn't want to do it he'd enjoy raping me. Watch closely what happens now.'

On the screen Nola wrenched her arm free with such force that she tumbled off the bed.

Wisdom, too, rolled off the bed to the floor and reached

for her. But Nola was too quick for him. She was on her feet and ran quickly around to the other side of the bed where she started gathering her clothes.

Wisdom was soon on his feet again and moving around the bed towards her in a threatening manner.

'He said to get dressed if I wanted to because then he could have the fun of ripping my clothes off before he had me again. I was very frightened.'

Donald asked; 'But why did you stay there? While he was on the floor you could have got away if you'd tried.'

'What? Run outside like that ... in the nude. I had to get something on before I went anywhere.'

On the screen Wisdom had taken Nola by her upper arms and by sheer strength he pushed her backwards so that she fell onto the bed with him in pursuit.

But Nola was determined on resistance. She raised her legs, knees bent, and placed both feet against Wisdom's chest then kicked her legs out violently.

The force of the kick sent Wisdom stumbling back to the right of the screen and out of camera range.

Nola climbed off the bed and began dressing hastily.

It was only only minutes before she too disappeared from the screen, now dressed, in the direction Wisdom had taken.

Nola pressed the remote and the picture froze, showing an empty room. 'That's it,' she said. 'He hit his head on the base of that washstand and he was still out to it when I left the unit.'

Hodgkiss asked. 'Is that the end of the recording?'

Nola frowned. 'Yes I think so. I don't think there's any more on this disc.'

Hodgkiss continued. 'Well I always think of those often revealing occasions when someone thinks a recording session has finished when the cameras were still rolling.'

'So you want me to keep playing the disc. That's easily done,' said Nola, pressing the remote again.

Nothing on the screen changed except the counter where the numbers began to advance rapidly.

Barely a minute had passed when Donald said. 'OK, that's enough. Let's get going. We've got work to do.'

'Just give it another minute or two,' said Hodgkiss. 'You never know your luck.'

'I know mine,' Donald muttered, *sotto voce*.

Nola turned to Hodgkiss. 'Just say when to stop.'

The words were scarcely out of her mouth when Angela Bly appeared from the right hand edge of the picture. In her left hand she carried a brown belt, its buckle trailing on the carpet.

She turned to face the way she had entered. She waved, she beckoned.

Then, after looking once around the room, she crossed to the bed, stooped and picked up something from under the bedside table. A ring. She slipped it on a finger, cocked her head to one side, admiring it.

She crossed once more to the centre of the room and stood, again beckoning towards the right edge of the screen.

Then she tossed the belt towards her right, paused, looked about the room then turned and disappeared in the direction she had come from.

Hodgkiss turned to Nola. 'Could you play that last bit again please ... from where she enters the room? There was something wrong ... something I don't understand.'

'What do you mean "wrong?"' Donald demanded. 'I didn't see anything wrong. It looked pretty straight forward to me. She was just getting rid of the murder weapon.'

'Murder weapon?' said Nola. 'You mean he was dead?'

Donald nodded. 'He was strangled ... probably with a belt. Probably the one she was carrying.'

'No doubt,' Hodgkiss snapped. 'But you could hardly say she was getting rid of it. If she'd wanted to be rid of it she'd have taken it away and burned it. Why just toss it across the room? Why leave it for the police to find ... and with her fingerprints on it? No. There was something very odd about what that woman did.'

'You're not suggesting, are you, that it wasn't her that did it ...murdered Wisdom?'

'I'm not suggesting anything, Donald, except that there was something very odd about that appearance of hers. And as for whether or not she killed the man ... you'd better get on and ask her. She's hardly going to deny she was there, is she? '

Donald waved a hand at the screen 'But all of that doesn't really prove much.'

'Is that what you think, is it? Really? I fancy a jury might find it very convincing ... together with statements from the people concerned.'

'Maybe. But it never showed the important bits ... like what was going on out of sight of the camera. We never saw Wisdom actually hitting his head on that washstand, and most important of all, we never saw the woman, or whoever it was, who actually throttling him with that belt ... it all happened out of sight of the camera.'

Hodgkiss shook his head. 'You don't demonstrate a great deal of confidence in your forensic officers, Donald. I'm sure they'll have no difficulty finding the culprit once they have examined the scene again. This time they will have a better idea of what to look and where to look for it ... I refer to the belt obviously. It appeared from what I could see to be brown in colour and rather thinner than most men's belts. Wouldn't you agree?'

'That's as may be, Dad. But it's all got to be done properly. A smart lawyer could have that whole video thrown out of court.' He turned to Sergeant Sanderson. 'Get in touch with her ... Angela Bly ... and arrange to interview her ASAP. Take a statement. Tell her about that if you like,' said Donald waving an arm at the screen which was now blank, 'and see what she has to say about it.'

Hodgkiss held up hand. 'Just one question please, Donald.' He turned to Nola. 'Would you kindly explain how you came by the film. And a second question if I may; had you left the building before Angela made her appearance on the screen?'

'Yes, I had. I saw her outside the building shortly after I left and she told me about how he usually video-ed what happened with his women in the bedroom. She said she'd check to see if there was a video with me in it and if so she'd take it and give it to me ... which she did. Otherwise he'd only hand it around to his mates to show how smart he is and how easy it is for him to get women.'

'Then she couldn't have played it through to the end,' said Donald. 'She wouldn't have wanted anyone to see her there with the belt in her hand, would she? That drops here right in it.'

'Nonsense, Donald,' said Hodgkiss. 'What on earth makes you think that? Her appearing on the screen holding the belt is not necessarily damning. She could have found it somewhere else in the unit ... in the hall, in the kitchen ... anywhere. She could have simply picked it up and carried it back to the bedroom to put it away.

'And another thing: don't forget when Mrs Tracey left the unit she left the front door open for the ambulance people who she was planning to call. Anyone could have strayed in and killed the ghastly man. God knows there must have been dozens of people with strong enough motives.'

'You've got an explanation for everything, haven't you,' Donald snapped. He turned to Nola and Gordon. 'And I want you two down at the station ... now.'

Gordon asked; 'D'you mind if we have another drink before we go?"

'So long as you're not driving' said Donald.

*　　*　　*

Angela Bly was not surprised when Wisdom called early telling her to come to work at his unit instead of the office in the St James Centre. Often she worked from the unit two or three days a week since most of Wisdom's mail went to his home unit and he kept all of his company records and correspondence there as well.

Angela had recognised the sense of this arrangement since his coffee shops were spread across the metropolitan area and his home was a convenient hub.

And she suspected, too, that when she arrived he would almost certainly demand she have sex with him, a demand she would meet very unwillingly.

Angela was finding it increasingly difficult to adopt a casual attitude towards her employer's affairs. While she had little sympathy for the procession of women, some of them quite young ... teenagers ... who found their ways to Wisdom's bed, his attitude towards women now disgusted her.

In a recent conversation with William Berger she had heard of some of the deplorable tactics Wisdom used to ensnare young girls. Berger had told her of two of the women who worked in one of his coffee shops who had been propositioned by Wisdom. One of them had gone to his unit when threatened with dismissal if she refused, and the other had left the job rather than comply.

Those two, Berger had told her, were just the tip of an

iceberg. At a recent meeting of four of the local coffee shop licensees he had heard similar stories of Wisdom's attempts, mostly successful to prey on young staff members.

Then William had told her why Wisdom was determined to evict the Bergers from their three shops rather than allow then time to make up their arrears. Esther had been standing outside the shop where she usually worked, waiting at a bus stop. Wisdom had stopped in his sports car and offered to drive here wherever she was going.

Esther had been uneasy about the offer but decided it would not be politic to refuse.

Once she was in the car Wisdom had driven straight to a secluded spot in a nearby national park and demanded to have sex with her. When she refused he had simply pushed her out of the car and driven off.

She was without her mobile phone and faced an hour's walk back to the shop.

This incident appalled Angela more than anything she had heard so far. Really, someone should do something to stop the man.

She parked in a nearby side-street, got out and locked the car. She glanced at her watch. Corey had told her not to be too early as he had a special assignment to complete before she arrived.

Angela knew that the reference to a "special assignment" meant that he had a woman there and she should not arrive before the 'assignment' had been completed.

Damn him, she thought. There's enough work waiting

there to keep me busy for the rest of the day. His books are a mess and that accountant of his is worse than useless.

Why should I waste my time waiting around here while he's up there with some bimbo. She set off towards Wisdom's unit block, checking her handbag for the keys she'd need to get in in case Wisdom was too pre-occupied to come to the door.

As she arrived outside the block she saw an attractive woman of about forty standing on the kerb looking about anxiously as if waiting for someone to arrive.

Angela had never seen a good photograph of Nola Tracey, but in spite of that she felt sure that this was her.

The only photo she'd seen of Nola was on one of Wisdom's phones. The photo was of Nola and a man, her husband no doubt, taken at night-time in the bush. In the photo the two were standing side by side, looking down at a third person, it looked like a woman in nightclothes, lying on the ground.

Perfect blackmail material, Angela had thought. That's probably what brought her here today.

Well, there's one way to find out, although she'll probably say it's none of my business.

As she approached Angela held out a hand. 'Nola, is it? Nola Tracey?'

Then she saw the livid finger marks on Nola's forearm. She pointed at them. 'Did he do that?' he asked. 'Wisdom? It's all right you can tell me. I might work for the brute, but I've got no time for him.'

Nola said. 'The so-and-so threatened to rape me but I

managed to push him over and get away. I'm just going to ring the ambulance.'

'The ambulance? What ever for? What happened?'

'When I kicked him away he stumbled and hit his head on the bottom of the washstand. He was still out to it when I got away. I left the door open so they could get in.'

'Good for you? If you haven't rung the ambulance yet just hold off a minute. Let me go up and have a look at him. He's pretty tough. He'll probably only need a panadol and a bandage. Was he bleeding much?'

'No. Hardly at all.'

'Then he'll probably be fine. If he really needs help I'll get a doctor to him. There's a retired GP lives in the building. He'll fix him up for a small fee.'

Just then a car stopped at the kerb, the driver leaned over and opened the passenger's door.

'My husband,' Nola explained. climbing into the car. She attached her seat belt then lowered the window. 'He told me that he'd made a video of what happened up there. I'd be very grateful if you could somehow wipe it without getting into bother. I'd hate to think it was floating around.'

'That's par for the course with him,' Angela said bitterly. 'Don't worry about it. I know where the machine is. I'll send you the disc ... or better still I'll drop it off. You should have it in case he turns nasty and you need to take some sort of action against him. If he wants to know what happened to it I'll just play dumb and say you must have found it and taken it with you. He just loves to show those things to his mates. He holds special porn evenings with them. He's a pig of a man.'

'One day he's going to get what he deserves,' said Nola. 'I don't know how you put up with him,' she said, then lowered the window.

Angela waved as the car drove away, then she hurried into the building.

*　　*　　*

Donald pushed back the door to Sanderson's office. 'Have you arranged to talk to the Bly woman yet?'

The sergeant looked up from his desk, leaving a finger on the page of a report he had been checking. 'I just got off the phone from her. She wasn't very happy about it. She said I'd already interviewed her once and wasn't that enough. I told her we had some new information that needed to be explained. I've got a feeling she might have known what I was talking about although she didn't ask. I'm seeing her at two o'clock at the office in Wisdom's unit.'

'At the unit?' Donald asked. 'What's she doing there? Is she moving in? Or perhaps he left it to her. Be interesting if he did and he'd already told her about it. People would have killed for much less. That place must be worth millions.'

Sanderson shook his head. 'I don't think it's anything like that. She said she'd decided to move in there because it was more convenient than trying to carry on from the other office. She reckons she'll do her best to keep the business running until the legal situation is sorted out and they know who inherits it. She didn't seem to know if he had any relatives who might be interested in taking over.'

'Do we know who Wisdom's solicitor is? He'd know all of that stuff … who inherits … who the relatives are? That's stuff we need to know … and as of now,'

'I expect she'll know who the solicitor is. She seems to handle all his correspondence. Oh, and I've asked the crime scene boys to have another look around on the basis of that video. They might think of some new places to look.'

'Yeah. Good idea. Now, when you go to interview her this afternoon were you thinking of taking Dad … Mr Hodgkiss … with you?'

'I'd thought about it but I decided I should be able to handle this one on my own. Do you want me to ask him along?'

Donald shrugged. 'I'll leave it to you, sergeant. But he'll want to know what she's had to say.'

'Then I'll send him a copy of her statement …. if that's OK with you, inspector.'

'It's fine with me, sergeant. Takes the heat of me. Now I'll be able to go home without him laying in wait for me with a hundred questions. If he's got any questions I'll just tell him to ring you. Right?'

Sergeant Sanderson nodded uncertainly.

The sergeant was edging his unmarked police car cautiously towards the exit of the crowed parking area at the back of the police station, when his phone, resting on the passenger's seat beside him, sounded his ringtone *Danny Boy*.

He glanced across. Hodgkiss' name was on the screen. He hesitated for a moment then reached over and opened the connection.

'I hope I'm not ringing too early,' Hodgkiss began quickly, 'but I wanted to catch you before you had your meeting with Ms Bly.'

Sergeant Sanderson shook his head in disbelief. The old guy's psychic, he thought. 'I'm just on my way there now, Mr Hodgkiss,' he said.

'Then I'm glad I caught you. I've had one or two thoughts I want to share with you before you met that lady. Do you have moment?'

'It's a bit awkward just now. Just a minute or two perhaps,' said the sergeant, stopping his car and completely blocking the narrow exit. 'Go ahead.'

'I won't keep you a minute,' Hodgkiss continued. 'I just thought that if you question Ms Bly about that video it may well be that she is unaware of her brief appearance on it carrying what Donald seems convinced is the murder weapon.'

The sergeant said. 'Yes, I thought about that too. I reckon she would never have handed over the disc to Mrs Tracey if she knew what was on it … not without wiping it first.'

'Precisely, sergeant,' said Hodgkiss. 'So since we can assume that she is unaware of her rather, um … suggestive appearance, it may be that she will be entirely frank when it comes to answering questions.'

'Exactly, Mr Hodgkiss. But if she knew about her appearance at the end of the disc she'd probably try to shift the blame onto Mrs Tracey which, in the circumstances, would be most unfair since she, that is Ms Tracey, apparently had no idea what was on the latter part of the video. I'd given the matter some thought and decided to show Ms Bly the relevant part of the video and tell her the circumstances in which we discovered it ... that you suggested we keep playing it beyond the point where Mrs Tracey thought it ended.'

'Good thinking, sergeant. Once she knows that Mrs Tracey didn't deliberately dob her in, I think is the vernacular, then she won't be tempted to shift the blame, thus confusing matters.'

'Is that all you wanted to tell me, Mr Hodgkiss.'

'Yes. If I think of anything else I'll ring. Whereabouts are you now?'

'I'm just leaving the station. Inspector Burke said I should send you a copy of Ms Bly's statement when I'm finished it;

'I shall look forward to seeing it sergeant, although ...'

There followed a short silence.

'Although what, Mr Hodgkiss? What's on your mind?'

'It just occurred to me that if I was actually with you when I had another thought that required explanation then it would be far more convenient than me having to ring and perhaps interrupting you in the middle of taking Ms Bly's statement.'

He hurried on before the sergeant could comment. 'Oh, and just one other thing that came to me last night.

Now that we have visual evidence of what took place in Mr Wisdom's bedroom it may be worthwhile recalling the scene-of-crime officers to have ...'

'... have another look,' the sergeant finished the sentence. 'Is that what you were going to say? If so, it's done, Mr Hodgkiss. I saw to it last night. They should be there a little later.' Sanderson left a short pause. 'I don't suppose you'd care to come along ... just for the ride?'

'I thought you'd never ask,' said Hodgkiss, 'Are you far away?'

'I'll be there in five,' said the sergeant.

Hodgkiss was waiting on the nature strip outside the Burke's bungalow when Sanderson drew up.

Sanderson reached over and opened the passenger's door. 'I don't suppose you thought of anything else while I was on the way?' he asked.

Hodgkiss climbed in. 'Actually I did,' he said, fastening his seat belt. 'You remember we asked Mrs Tracey who told her about the bloody footprint on the piece of tissue found under Mrs Connaught's bed?'

'Yes, I remember,' said the sergeant nodding his head vigourously. 'And I also remember that the conversation got side-tracked and she never told us who it was.'

'Quite right, sergeant. But it hardly matters though, does it. We know anyway, don't we?'

'Do we?' said Sergeant Sanderson, turning sharply to look at Hodgkiss. 'I think she'd only got as far as telling us who *didn't* tell her.'

'Yes, and the only one she hadn't mentioned was the person who *did* tell her ... Mr Berger.'

'Mr Berger? But what about Ms Bly? It could have been her.'

'Yes, possibly, but Ms Bly could only have known if Berger told her. And Berger must have heard it from James Connaught himself who was there when it was found. But Connaught never told him the details ... which foot and only the heel.'

'Yes, I see where you're going. But if that's true what's the point of it ... trying to work out how Mrs Tracey knew about it?'

'The point, sergeant, is that it demonstrates a connection between the Connaughts and the Bergers ... something Donald has denied all along.'

The sergeant nodded thoughtfully. 'Yes, that's true. And your suggestion that we check James Connaught's alibi for the time of Wisdom's death and Berger's for the time of Mrs Connaught's death would have made sense if they'd done it ... or rather set it up between them. But now we know that it was Mrs Tracy all along ... or possibly Ms Bly.'

'Yes, Sergeant, but isn't it as well to cross the Is and dot the Tees as we go along. Otherwise we end up in confusion ... as the inspector is inclined to from time to time. Don't you agree?'

'Oh definitely,' said the sergeant, pulling over and braking. 'Here we are. She's working from his unit ... or someone's unit.'

'Then you haven't spoken to his solicitor yet?' said Hodgkiss, undoing his seat belt. 'About Wisdom's testamentary arrangements?'

'Yes, I have, but he wouldn't tell me a thing. He said if I wanted to know to contact Ms Bly.'

'Do you mean he's told her what's in Wisdom's will?'

'I asked him that and all he'd say was to contact her. But he must have told her if she knows what's in it. Unless Wisdom told her or told someone else and they told her. But that's hardly likely.'

'Then we may assume that she is a beneficiary,' said Hodgkiss.

Sergeant Sanderson nodded. 'Which puts her in a difficult situation.'

'A *more* difficult situation,' Hodgkiss amended as they walked together towards the unit block. 'But we won't know until we have the details. After all, he might have left her only a derisory sum ... a few dollars. But somehow I don't see a fellow like Wisdom doing that. He struck me as an all-or-nothing sort of fellow.'

They took the lift up to find Angela waiting for them at the door to Wisdom's unit. She was not pleased to see them. 'I hope this is not going to take as long as the other day, Mr Sanderson. I have more work than I can handle in sorting things out here. I'm afraid Mr Wisdom did not leave his affairs in good order.'

'I'll take no longer than necessary, Ms Bly. But first may I introduce Mr Hodgkiss who is assisting me in this matter.'

The two shook hands tentatively. 'You're not by any chance a shorthand writer, are you,' Angela asked, hopefully, 'here to assist the sergeant? That would be extremely useful because he's not the fastest scribe in the business.'

'I'm afraid I'm not a shorthand writer, Ms Bly, although it is a skill I have always admired.' He turned to the sergeant. 'But if Mr Sanderson agrees I will be happy to make notes.'

'Thank you, Mr Hodgkiss, I'd appreciate that,' said Sanderson. 'Now, Ms Bly, there are several matters that I need to clear up immediately.'

'Several,' she repeated. 'I thought after your prolonged inquisition the other day you'd have had all the information you needed.'

'I understand that, Ms Bly, but there have been developments since then ... matters that require clarifying.'

'Developments. And what are these developments and matters?' Angela asked, more than a trace of anxiety in her voice.

'The first is the question of Mr Wisdom's will. I understand you are a beneficiary.'

'Who told you that?'she snapped.

'Is it true?' Sanderson persisted.

'I suggest you ask his solicitor. He's the proper person to ask.'

'I agree, and I asked him. But for some reason he refused to tell me and suggested that I ask you.'

'Well, I'm telling you to ask him. The man's a fool. He doesn't know what he's doing.'

Hodgkiss said. 'But you are a beneficiary, aren't you?'

When Angela stood, arms folded and mouth set in a tight defiant line Sergeant Sanderson decided to move on.

'Very well. Let's leave that for the time being. Now I wish to ask you about certain events that took place in this unit shortly before Mr Wisdom died, and afterwards. We believe that you are in a position to ...'

'I know ... assist you with your inquiries. Very well, sergeant. Let's get on with it. Now, what are these developments?'

'They can be best illustrated if you have a CD player handy.'

'A CD player. Really. Then may I assume you've seen the video of Mr Wisdom and Mrs Tracey ... the one I gave her?'

'That's correct, Ms Bly.'

'Then there's no need to play it for me. I've already seen it. I played it before I dropped it off to her place. It was just the same awful stuff he got up to with all the women who came here. There's nothing new on it except the poor woman.'

Detective Sanderson shook his head roguishly. 'I think you're wrong there, Ms Bly. I don't think you've seen this one ... not *all* of it.'

'What do you mean not *all* of it?' I played it through right to the end ... right to where Mrs Tracey got dressed and left.'

Hodgkiss nodded. 'That's what we thought, Mrs Bly. However, if you'd kept playing the disc you'd have seen more ... the part we need to ask you about.'

Angela shrugged. 'Very well then, if you must. Come through to the office. There's a machine there.'

In the office Angela slipped the disc into a player, turned on a TV set on the wide, cluttered desk, and pressed a remote.

Wisdom's bedroom appeared on the screen.

Sanderson said; 'I don't think we need to go through all the depressing preliminaries with Mrs Tracey. Would you fast forward to the point where Mrs Tracy leaves the room, please?'

The figures moved with rapid jerky movements until Nola Tracey, now fully dressed, exited to the right of the picture.

Angela pressed the stop button. 'That's it' she said. 'The end.'

'No, not at all,' said Sanderson. 'Keep going, but at normal speed.'

The screen seemed frozen except for the counter which started to tick over in real time.

'And how long does this go on?' Angela asked impatiently.

'Not long' said Sanderson. 'Keep going. I'm sure you'll agree it's worth the wait.'

Minutes passed then Angela entered the bedroom from the right of the screen. In her hand she carried a belt which trailed on the carpet. She appeared agitated. She looked about. She crossed to the bed, stooped, picked up an object, a ring, put it on a finger, admired it, then turned and walked back to the centre of the room. She stood ... she looked about ... she waved her arms in a beckoning fashion

Abruptly she tossed the belt out of sight towards the right hand edge of the screen.

Hodgkiss asked quietly. 'Why did you do that?'

'Why did I do what?' Angela asked.

'Throw the belt away like that?'

'I've no idea really. I'd found it somewhere and I'd just been carrying it around.'

'Yes, so we saw,' said Hodgkiss 'Where was it when you found it?'

'Really I've no idea, Mr Hodgkiss. You can hardly expect me to remember a detail like that ... , not in view of all that's happened since.'

'Perhaps not,' Hodgkiss concede. 'But why didn't you put it away in the one of the wardrobes in the bedroom? That's where it would have been kept normally, isn't it?'

Angela nodded. 'I really wouldn't know. I wasn't the man's valet and the truth is that I'd become sick and tired of being Mr Wisdom's general all purpose factotum ... his permanent on-call slave. He was dead. I didn't give a damn about him or any of his neckties or belts or anything else he happened to own. I was over him ... totally over him. Do you understand?'

'Perfectly, Ms Bly,' said Hodgkiss. 'Now just one more question if you don't mind?'

Ms Bly sighed wearily. 'Yes, Mr Hodgkiss What is it now?'

'Just a purely technical request. Do you know how to use the zoom facility on this machine? There is something I wish to see in greater detail.'

Angela nodded. 'Yes, I can do that, Mr Hodgkiss. What do you want me to zoom in on.'

'Your mouth, Ms Bly. You see among my many modest accomplishments is a talent for lip reading and I noticed that from the moment you entered the room you were speaking in a quite agitated fashion. I do not believe that you were talking to yourself, so naturally I wonder who on earth you *were* talking to. Whoever it was they were not visible on the screen, but judging from the manner in which you threw the belt I would say that this person ... possibly an accomplice ... was not far out of the camera's range ... probably near the ensuite door. And I have no doubt that this accomplice had been briefed to take the belt away and dispose of it. What do you say to that, Ms Bly?'

'I say it's a load of nonsense,' Angela snapped.

'Is it? Then perhaps you can tell us where the belt is, because so far as I am aware the police who made a thorough search of this unit haven't located it.'

'Well don't blame me if they're not up to the job. And if you want to zoom in on my mouth you can do it yourself if you're so damn clever.'

She moved quickly to the player and ejected the disc.

But Sergeant Sanderson had anticipated her. He stepped forward quickly, elbowed her to one side and took the disc when it slid out.

Angela favoured both men with poisonous glances, then

turned and left the room. Moments later they heard the front door slam shut.

'Do you really know how to lip-read, Mr Hodgkiss,' Sanderson asked, as he slipped the disk into a plastic cover.

'Not very well I'm afraid, sergeant. All I know about lip reading is that it is a most inexact science, but if you know something about the context of the conversation you might get some words right and perhaps even reconstruct the gist of a conversation. Otherwise it's usually fifty percent guesswork. However, I *do* know that the person who I believe is the off-screen presence in that scene has a name that demands particular contortions of both the lips and the tongue. So an experienced lip reader should be able to pick it up. And I believe our police have access to lip readers so there is at least an outside chance that if Ms Bly said the name that should give us a fresh field to till.'

'Well, I hope we can find someone to come up with the name of this off-screen character you think she was talking to,' said Sanderson, 'because I don't have the least idea who you're talking about.'

'Really, Sergeant, I'd've thought it was obvious,' said Hodgkiss.

Sanderson shook his head. 'Not to me I'm afraid, Mr Hodgkiss. But if you don't want to tell me ...'

Hodgkiss held up a hand. 'I have no objection to telling *you*, Sergeant, but it must go no further. Understood.'

'Understood,' the sergeant repeated. For some reason the

old fellow didn't want Donald to know that he'd solved it. Or perhaps he wouldn't want him to know in case he turned out to be wrong which, going on past performances, did not seem at all likely.

Hodgkiss leaned over and spoke quietly into Sanderson's ear.

Sanderson's eyes widened in surprise. Then he nodded. 'Yes. That makes sense. But I'd never have thought of that.'

There was a heavy knock on the front door.

'That'll be the scene-of-crime boys now,' said the sergeant. 'If you're right they should have no trouble finding finger-prints to prove it ... one way or the other.'

'It's the fingerprints on the belt that will interest me most,' said Hodgkiss. 'And I have more than a vague idea where it may be found.'

*   *   *

Inspector Donald Burke looked down at the sheaf of papers on his desk, stapled neatly together in the top left hand corner.

It was the sergeant's latest report on the tricky double murder they were investigating and it contained words the inspector had never before seen in print, let alone understood.

This is what I get for encouraging him to talk to Dad about the case, he thought ruefully.

But having encouraged the collaboration how could he

end it, particularly now the two were coming up with some interesting results.

But this business about finding an expert in lip reading that Sanderson had suggested in this latest report … that had his father-in-law' fingerprints all over it.

Donald re-read the relevant paragraphs.

'I am in no doubt that Ms Bly's precipitate attempt to take possession of the disc in question was driven by fear that it had the potential to reveal her central role in the affair. I say this because when Mr Hodgkiss asked her if she could operate a zoom feature on the television she seemed at first happy to comply. Then when he stated specifically that he wanted to apply the zoom feature to her mouth Ms Bly appeared at first a little confused, as was I. It was not until he mentioned his talent for lip reading that Ms Bly realised what was the object of his inquiry. That was when she took immediate steps to take possession of the disc. Luckily I was able to forestall her. Her precipitate action was in my view a strong indication of her concern at what a competent lip reader may be able to reveal about her part in this affair.

Mr Hodgkiss is of the opinion that the police department may be in a position to obtain the services of a lip reading expert who could look at the disc and perhaps reveal what Ms Bly was saying to the person she was addressing at the time but who was not 'in shot', which

I understand is the phrase used in the world of film production. There is no doubt that it would greatly assist our inquiry if this could be done as the person to whom she tossed the belt may turn out to be very much involved in the crime, possibly even as the perpetrator.

Further Mr Hodgkiss said that his understanding is that lip reading is not an exact science and if the department obtained the services of such a specialist it would be of considerable assistance to the process if that person knew in advance a little about the likely context of the conversation. By way of assisting, Mr Hodgkiss has given a brief outline of what he regards is very likely that context. He is particularly interested in any Proper Names that Ms Bly may have spoken, although he warned that she may not have spoken the name of the person who was with her because this would be usual in the circumstances.

Donald lowered his head into his hands. He had no doubt where this extraordinary idea had come from. Lateral thinking, he would call it, or thinking outside the square. Two phrases Donald had come to detest.

But that last sentence … what on earth did it mean? 'She may not have spoken the name of the person who was with her because this would be usual in the circumstances.'

He had sent a copy of the sergeant's report to his superior officer, Superintendent O'Hare, who, to his amazement, had enthused at the idea of calling in a lip reader and had already arranged for an expert in the art to call the following morning to start work. The expert had advised that he would be able to assist more effectively if he could be given the likely context of the conversation he was to view and some background.

And there it was ... the context and some background. Hodgkiss had already written it and that too had gone to the superintendent.

He turned his attention once more to the report.

TO WHOM IT MAY CONCERN
Some notes on the vision of the video under consideration.

The video shows a part of the bedroom of Mr Corey Wisdom, deceased. His corpse is not visible but it is in the area off the screen to the right. The female who enters the room is Ms Angela Bly, an employee of the deceased. She is the only person to appear during the period under review, although it is apparent that there is another person within ear-shot since she is seen to be talking, sometimes in an animated fashion, accompanied by gestures. The identity of this other person is not known, and to identify him or her is the chief object of this exercise.

So to assist I will provide a list of the names of all those involved in this investigation since it seems likely that the subject, Ms Bly, will have spoken one or more of these during the course of her soliloquy:

William Berger

Esther Berger, wife of William

James Connaught

Phyllis Connaught, (deceased) wife of James

Grattan Tracey

Nola Tracey (wife of Grattan) very much alive.

The situation on the screen I can confidently assert came about like this; Mr Wisdom called Ms Bly and asked her to come to his unit to work rather than at his usual office in St James. A check of phone records tends to confirm that this is the case. Ms Bly said that when she arrived Mr Wisdom did not answer the door. She deemed this to be not unusual since he frequently has women staying with him there. So she used keys of her own to enter. She found his body in the bedroom about midway between the door to the bedroom's ensuite bathroom and a second door that led to the main hall of the unit. Ms Bly insists that she did not touch the body but found a thin leather belt laying beside it. She picked this up and is seen carrying it on the video. One wonders why a very worldly person such as Ms Bly seemed unaware of the evidential importance of the belt and that touching it would have seriously contaminated the crime scene. I have no doubt that during the course of her rather animated discussion with the party off-screen she would have referred to the belt — particularly as she tossed it in what was almost certainly the direction of her interlocutor. I note that she tossed it at about chest height so that he or she to whom it was directed would have caught it in a reflex action, thus their fingerprints would be on it, probably superimposed over hers. Was this a deliberate ploy on her part? She is a highly intelligent woman and I am convinced that this could have been a deliberate manoeuvre.

If you feel I can be of further assistance I will be pleased to make myself available at short notice.

Edgar Hodgkiss (Police Consultant.)

"Police Consultant." Donald ground his teeth. Next thing he'll be on the bloody payroll. This has got to end, he promised himself. But how? Already the superintendent was going along with everything Hodgkiss put forward.

He glanced at his watch. The lip reading genius the superintendent had dug up from somewhere would be arriving any minute to look over the video. Well, let's hope he comes up with a big fat zero. That'll take a bit of wind out of the old troublemaker's sails, then perhaps I'll be able to get this investigation back on track ... back to normal.

He pushed back from his desk, took the video disc from his top drawer and headed down the corridor to the room the superintendent had ask him to set up for the viewing.

Donald shared the policeman's natural antipathy for experts. In his view they were usual overqualified with irrelevant information and over endowed with egos. Not only that, they were more likely to come up with stuff that, far from helping, often damaged the police case.

The specimen awaiting for him did nothing to improve his opinion; short, bearded, seriously overweight, smoking in defiance of the multiple signs on the walls and wearing sneakers without socks.

The superintendent, chatting amiably with the fellow, appeared to have overlooked these many failings although he was even now fanning the fellow's cigarette smoke away from his face in a futile attempt to avoid passive smoking.

He looked up when Donald entered. 'Ah. Good,' he said 'Now we can get the show on the road.'

He introduced Donald to Felix Fender who offered a limp, damp hand which Donald touched briefly without making eye contact.

Felix put out the offending hand once more and Donald placed the disc in it. 'This may take a little while,' said Felix. 'So there's need for the two of you to hang around unless you've got nothing better to do. But you might have to send along that Hodgkiss fellow who wrote the report. He might be a bit of help if I get stuck. I'll let you know if I need him.'

'I doubt if he's at the station right now' said the superintendent, 'but we can send a car for him if necessary. He doesn't live far away.'

Not nearly far enough, Donald thought.

'Fine,' said Felix. 'Now, if you'll both excuse me.' He made sweeping motions, urging them towards the door.'

Donald needed no encouragement.

In the corridor he turned to the superintendent. 'I hope we're not paying that fellow too much.' he said.

The superintendent nodded. 'So do I,' he said. 'But it'll be worth it if he *does* manage to come up with something. I've still no idea who we're looking for here. Have you, Donald?'

'I've got certain ideas about it, but it's early days yet,' Donald said, hoping that the superintendent wouldn't require details of his 'certain' ideas.

But the superintendent's thoughts were moving on another path. 'I hope Edgar's at home this morning in case that fellow wants to consult him.'

'Don't worry about that, superintendent, 'He'll be waiting by the phone.'

Ten minutes later Donald was sitting at his desk, still seething at the indignity of being ordered out by that fat little fraud before the viewing began.

Sergeant Sanderson had come to the door and asked how the lip reading was progressing. This had not improved Donald's mood. He had shrugged and attempted to make light of it. 'Nothing yet,' he said, 'and I'm not waiting around holding my breathe to see if he actually comes up with anything worth knowing.'

Sanderson had nodded agreement and disappeared in the direction of his office.

But the worst came about half an hour later when Donald happened to look out of his widow in time to see a cab stop in the courtyard below and Hodgkiss get out.

'I might have known it,' he fumed. 'I just knew he'd get into the act somehow.'

Then Sergeant Sanderson appeared at his door once more

in a state of some excitement. 'I saw Mr Hodgkiss just arrive in a taxi. Do you know what happened, inspector? Did the lip reading fellow ask for him?'

'I've no idea, sergeant,' said Donald, without looking up from the Neighbourhood Watch report which had been sitting unread in his in tray for weeks. 'If they come up with anything of interest I expect the superintendent will let us know in due course.'

Donald returned his attention to the problems of neighbourhood watch. But after more than half an hour he became aware that he was reading the same paragraph multiple times.

Then the sound of another vehicle entering the courtyard caught his attention. He stood, crossed to the window and looked down in time to see Hodgkiss and the lip reading expert exit the back of the building and walk towards a waiting cab.

The lip reader pulled a door open, stood talking to Hodgkiss, then after delivering a friendly pat on the upper arm, climbed into the cab and slammed the door.

The cab drove off with the expert waving through a lowered widow and Hodgkiss waving energetically in return.

Donald shook his head. Best of mates now, apparently. But did they come up with anything worth knowing? Bet they didn't, he thought hopefully. Well I expect I'll soon now if they have.

* * *

Hodgkiss was enjoying a mug of black tea on the back deck when Esme pushed back the sliding door from the family room and stepped out.

'Phone for you, Dad. Superintendent O'Hare. Something to do with lip reading. Why would he be ringing you about that? You don't know anything about lip reading.'

'Don't I?' asked Hodgkiss. 'Maybe you're right. I don't remember.'

Esme shook her head as she handed him the phone. I should be used to those sort of strange remarks from him, she thought as she watched him hold the phone to his ear, listening. Then he simply nodded his head once and said: 'Five minutes. Fine.'

He pushed back his bench seat and rose. 'Apparently I *do* know something about lip reading,' he said as he headed for the family room door. 'I must, because there's an expert on the subject wants to consult me. Mr O'Hare is sending a car.'

The unmarked police car deposited Hodgkiss in the internal courtyard of the police station where O'Hare was waiting to meet him.

'This expert fellah read your notes, Edgar,' he said. 'Now he wants to have a talk to you about it to clear up a few points. I hope you can help us on this one, because at the moment we're getting nowhere fast.'

'I think I should be able to sort it out for you this morning, superintendent. That video should tell us all we need to know. Meanwhile there's something that needs to be done without delay.'

'Oh,. And what's that, Edgar?'

'The belt. We must get possession of that,'

'No argument there, Edgar. But the problem is what did they do with it … whoever it was. Where is the thing? Have you any idea?'

'I think you'll find Mr Berger has it,' said Hodgkiss, 'although he may have disposed of it by now. But even if he has it should not be too hard to find. Sergeant Sanderson knows where the Bergers live.'

'Fine. I'll send him there as soon as I've set you up with this Felix fellah.'

Felix was obviously relieved to see Hodgkiss. As soon as the two were alone Felix said: 'Glad to see you, Edgar. I'm getting nowhere with this damned business. Can you think of anything else about it that might give me a clue what to look for?'

Hodgkiss shook his head. 'I doubt if it will be necessary to look for anything more. I have just one question: you have the list of names I gave of people who the woman may have mentioned during her rant?'

Yes,' said Felix. 'I paid special attention to all the names she said. In fact she said most of the names on your list.'

'Most of them. But not all'?

'No. She missed out just one name; that fellow Berger. Everyone else on the list she mentioned although it's not easy to make much sense of what she was saying about them. Unfortunately I had only the back of her head most of the time.'

'No matter,' said Hodgkiss. 'You've told me all I need to know, thank you, Felix. Now perhaps we should collaborate on a report for the superintendent to fully justify our joint effort here this morning. What do you say?'

Felix smiled broadly. 'I was about to suggest something like that but didn't have the nerve.'

The two settled amicably side by side at a battered laminate-topped table. Felix produced a lap top from a bag and, by agreement, Hodgkiss began to dictate slowly. It was not a lengthy document. Ten minutes later they printed it from a computer in the next room and Hodgkiss took the original to an adjoining office where he prevailed on a young woman to make three copies.

Felix rang for a taxi and Hodgkiss accompanied him downstairs and into the courtyard to make their farewells.

Now for the tricky part, Hodgkiss thought, as he headed for the superintendent's office armed with the report.

*   *   *

Esme was not amused when Hodgkiss arrived home to inform her of arrangements he had for later that day. 'You just turn up here and announce without a word of warning that you expect me to feed and water all these people at the drop of a hat ... and some of them total strangers, too.'

Hodgkiss raised a hand in what was intended to be a placatory gesture. 'If it's to much trouble for you, Esme, if you fell you can't cope, I will take them down to the coffee shop on the corner when they arrive, and ...'

'And spend a hundred dollars on them, because that's what it'll cost you at the prices they charge at that place. Anyone'd think that the price of coffee beans had actually trebled in the past month the way those people charge.'

Hodgkiss protested. 'It won't be *that* expensive. Besides, all these people will require is a cup of tea and a few biscuits. If that's too much for you to prepare, then ...'

'Is that what you think, is it, Dad. A cup of tea and a few biscuits. That's nonsense and you know it. If that's all I gave your friends when they turn up I'd never hear the end of it. Nowhere near good enough. I've been there before. You always expect the full treatment when you arrive home here with these sort of people.'

'And what exactly do you mean by "these soft of people?"'

'You know exactly what I mean ... people you've been interviewing. Suspects.' Then an alarming thought occurred to her. 'You haven't invited the murderer here, have you, Dad?'

Hodgkiss shook his head. 'No, Esme. No murderer, I promise you. Actually I don't know where the murderer is at the moment. I expect Donald is still looking for her.'

'Her? You mean it's a woman?'

'Yes, very much a woman. A most attractive one in fact.'

'It's not the one Donald told me about, is it; the one that gets around half naked all the time and with nothing on her feet?'

'Mrs Tracey, you mean? No. She won't be coming today,

although I will have to speak with her again in the near future to clarify some details. She is unfortunately not without blame in these unhappy events, but she certainly didn't murder anyone. In fact she was lucky not to have been murdered herself.'

'Well, I can tell you that Donald thinks she did it ... one of these murders.'

'I dare say, but as we both know Donald is not always right, is he?'

'There's no need to start on that, Dad. And I suppose you helped him with all this, did you?'

'Sergeant Sanderson and I did much of the spade work, yes.'

'You sure it was only the spade work? He will get the credit for it, won't he when you solve ... when it's solved.' She hurried on. 'And is the superintendent coming today, do you know?'

'I couldn't say for certain, Esme, but Sergeant Sanderson and I have been keeping him fully informed on all our inquiries. I expect he will be sufficiently interested to hear our conclusions.'

'Then if he does come I want you to promise me right now that you won't try to take all the credit as usual and leave Donald with egg on his face and without a word to say for himself.'

Hodgkiss frowned. 'Esme, I deeply resent your statement that I "take all the credit as usual". That is unfair and untrue as you would concede if you reflected on it for more than a moment.'

Esme shook her head. 'Maybe that's how *you* remember it, but *I* can remember that happening in the past ... and more than once. And it's certainly how Donald remembers it.'

'No doubt, but Donald is quite mistaken if he thinks Mrs Tracey is responsible for either of the murders, so it may be necessary for me to correct him if he persists in that view. In fact not only did she not commit murder but she was lucky to escape with her life when one of her supposed victims attacked her savagely.'

'What had she done?'

'She was stealing some jewellery from a ghastly woman who had gone out of her way to humiliate her.'

'Well, I say she probably deserved it. Now, where do you plan to put all these people when they arrive ... out on the deck or in the family room?'

'I think it looks like rain so inside might be safer.'

'Then you'd better get some more chairs, hadn't you, with all those people coming.'

'There won't be *that* many people, Esme. There will be the sergeant and the lip reading fellow and one other who will probably be a little late.'

'Oh, and who'll that be ... the one coming late?' Donald demanded, coming in through the door from the laundry.

'That will be Mr Berger,' said Hodgkiss. 'He was at first unwilling to accept my invitation until I assured him that he would not be facing arrest.'

'Oh did you?' said Donald. 'You told him he wouldn't be

facing arrest. Well I wouldn't've assured him of anything of the sort. In fact I think it's highly likely that I'll arrest him the moment he shows his face here. So perhaps you'd better ring him up and warn him before he leaves home. I suppose you know Sanderson found the belt at his place.'

'No, Donald, but I assumed that's where it would be. That's why I suggested Sanderson visit Mr Berger; to insist that he hand it over. Apparently he complied. But notwithstanding that I am confident that you won't arrest him … not once you are in possession of all the facts.'

'So you reckon you know it all, do you? The full story. Is that it? Well I certainly hope so because the superintendent cancelled all his afternoon appointments to be here to listen to what you've got to say, and he won't be impressed if it turns out to be a damp squid.'

'Damp *squib* I think is the phrase, Donald … a damp squib is a firework that fails to perform. Not a sea creature. But I doubt very much if the Superintendent will be disappointed with the outcome the lip reader and I reached.'

'And how how much use *was* that Felix fellow? D'you know how much he's charging for a few hour's work … six hundred dollars.'

Hodgkiss shrugged. 'I expect that's the going rate for a professional these days.'

'Professional!' Donald barked. 'Professional bull-shit artist … that's what that fellow is.'

'Language, Donald,' Esme rebuked quietly.

Donald continued. 'You're not going to defend the fellah,

are you, Dad? Did he really help ... did he actually contribute anything? Now tell us the truth.'

Hodgkiss thought about that. 'I think I could say with total honesty that the man is the fastest, most accurate two finger typist I've ever had the privilege to observe.'

'Yeah, and that's about all he was good at, right? Did he actually contribute something worthwhile with his lip reading or was that all a washout?'

Hodgkiss nodded. 'Yes, he did contribute something, come to think of it.'

'Really? And what was that? Apart from his typing?'

'You will have the opportunity to ask him yourself, Donald, as I expect him to arrive shortly. But to answer your question: among other things he told me that Ms Bly, during the course of her animated performance on the disc, spoke all but one of the names on the list I had provided in advance.'

'And that helped? Really? How?'

'It was very useful, even vital, although in a negative way. But let's wait until the others arrive. They shouldn't be too long now. Then I'll explain what I mean by that.'

For the next hour Hodgkiss sat in the Captain's chair at the desk in his bedroom at the front of the house and thought through the dramatic events of the past few days and how best to handle the next hour or so.

He was quite satisfied with the way his investigation had gone and his collaboration with Sergeant Sanderson, with Donald's qualified blessing, had proved fruitful.

But this in itself had created a problem. Now, to avoid upsetting Esme, he must find a way to present the case without taking all the spotlight away from Donald. That was his biggest challenge, not his explanation of the facts.

He picked up his phone and sent a short text message to the sergeant: VITAL TO STRESS IMPORTANCE OF DONALD'S INPUT.

The sergeant's reply was swift and cryptic: '?'

*　*　*

Donald and the superintendent were the first to arrive, parking their unmarked police cars one behind the other in the driveway at the side of the house.

In the kitchen Mr O'Hare took Esme in a bear hug in his enormous arms and planted kisses on both cheeks. 'Always great to see you Esme,' he said. 'I just don't get here often enough.' He looked around expectantly. 'Where's the resident genius hiding?'

From the corner of an eye Esme saw Donald flinch and look away in disgust.

'In his bedroom I expect,' said Esme. 'He'll be out shortly.'

Then the front doorbell rang and Esme hurried to the hall in time to see her father open the door to a short, rotund man. The two shook hands and smiling conspiratorially.

Their heads moved together for a brief but intense conversation.

'That's the lip reading fellah' said Donald over Esme's

shoulder. 'A real phony if ever I saw one.'

'Let's not be too hasty,' the superintendent cautioned. 'I read his report and ...'

'Dad's report, you mean,' Donald corrected. 'You could tell that from some of the words in it.'

'Well, whoever wrote it made a pretty fair job of working out what that woman was saying to whoever it was she was saying it to.'

'Maybe,' Donald conceded. 'But it was all old stuff ... stuff we knew about anyway ... who saw who and where ... what they did. None of it really got us any further ahead. Not that I can see.'

'Well, let's see what Edgar can make of it, eh?' said the superintendent. 'Here they come now.'

After the introductions were made they settled in the family room with a promise of afternoon tea in half an hour.

Settled comfortably in one of the wingback chairs Superintendent O'Hare announced: 'I had to cancel some pretty heavy appointments to come here this afternoon, Edgar. One of them, a back-bencher who's convinced that he's premier material, got quite shirty when I told him our meeting was off. He wanted to know what could possibly have been more important than a meeting with him.'

Hodgkiss shook his head. 'That must have sorely tested your tolerance, but I think between the three of us — Sergeant Sanderson, when he arrives, which I hope will be shortly — Felix here and I will provide you with enough ammunition to convince anyone, potential premier or not, that your presence here was the proper priority.'

'OK, Dad,' said Donald. 'Spare us the chatter because there's still a lot of work to be done before this business is properly tidied up. So exactly what did you and the king of lip readers actually come up with apart from all that old stuff in your report that we already knew about?'

Hodgkiss pushed up from the settee. 'Yes, Donald. I acknowledge that much of the material in our report was already in your hands. I grant you that. What is new is our interpretation of that material.'

He turned to face the superintendent. 'Looking at that video it seemed to me that the most important question it posed was this: who was the person standing 'out of shot', as they say … probably in the hall just outside the bedroom … while Ms Bly was holding forth and gesturing in a manner that I interpreted as an invitation for that person to enter the room and therefore be seen on the video.

'But whoever it was they resisted her siren call. But why? Perhaps they were disturbed by Ms Bly's agitated state of mind, or they may have felt uncomfortable at having to pass close to Mr Wisdom's body which they must have seen if they were standing near the hall door.

'I couldn't ask Ms Bly who it was because she was not and still is not available for questioning.'

He turned to Donald. 'I take it that is still the position.'

Donald nodded. 'We'll find her. Don't worry about that.'

Hodgkiss continued 'So in her absence I adopted the rather unusual course of suggesting that the department seek the services of a lip reader.'

Here Hodgkiss sketched a bow in Felix's direction. Felix waved a shy hand in acknowledgment.

'And a fat lot of use that was.' Donald muttered under his breath.

But Hodgkiss had caught the remark. 'Perhaps it was a little more use than you think.'

'Oh. And how was that? I've seen the report you and him cobbled together and there's absolutely nothing new in it or anything that gets us any further ahead.'

Hodgkiss raised a cautionary finger. 'I would not agree with that for one moment. I think Felix's interpretation of part of the monologue is most revealing ... the part where Ms Bly, on several occasions invites the person 'out of shot' to 'come and see for yourself' is significant when taken together with her actions.'

'Oh and what was so clever about that? Any one could see she was trying to get someone to come into the room so they could be identified.'

'And you think it is not important to have evidence to confirm that? Just have patience, Donald. I've told you that it's a matter of interpretation of the know facts. So let us look at it one step at a time.

'Remember, I provided Felix with a list of the names of those directly involved in the case: the Traceys, the Bergers and James Connaught, and asked him to note if Ms Bly spoke any of those names during her monologue.'

'Yeah, Dad We know all that. Now tell us something we

don't know.'

'Give the man a chance, Donald,' said the superintendent. 'He's hardly started.'

'Thank you, superintendent,' said Hodgkiss. 'Now, if Donald will contain himself for just a little while, let us look at Felix's imaginative reconstruction of Ms Bly's monologue. While parts of it are admittedly speculation, because he could not make out all of the words spoken, he is nevertheless quite sure that she spoke the names of all those people on my list with one exception ... William Berger.

'Now, Ms Bly knew the Bergers well. They operated three of Mr Wisdom's coffee shops, and she knew that Mr Wisdom had taken steps to deprive the Berger's of their livelihood because, due to the pandemic, their sales had dropped off to the point where their business was no longer viable although they had exhausted their own finances in trying to survive.

'She also knew the Traceys because Mr Wisdom had set her the task of tracking down Mrs Tracey. And the Connaughts she had heard of through her conversation with Mrs Tracey. In fact Felix is certain that she spoke the name Connaught more than once, and that one of those occasions was in conjunction with Christian name Phyllis, so perhaps she knew of that lady's fate and was referring to it for some reason ... perhaps in the context of a threat. You know the sort of thing ... The same thing could happen to you.'"

'That's just fantasy stuff, Dad,' said Donald. 'You seriously reckon any of that was worth $600. What's your point?'

'The point, Donald, is this: why did Ms Bly not speak William Berger's name? She spoke the names of all the others on my list — all those involved in our investigation. So why did she not say the name William Berger?'

'OK. She didn't say *William Berger*. So what?'

Hodgkiss stood for a moment, immobile, eyes closed. Then he continued quietly. 'Now, if one speaks the name *William* it requires the most lively and obvious movements of the lips and tongue, and yet Felix is sure that she never spoke the name and I am happy to take his word for it.

'So the question is why would Ms Bly not have spoken his name during what was, according to Felix's reconstruction of her monologue, a summary of all of those involved?'

'I've no idea,' said Donald, 'but I'm pretty sure you're going to tell us anyway.'

Hodgkiss shook his head angrily. 'Donald, your attitude in much of this investigation has done you little credit. It gives me no pleasure to speak like this in the present company. You appear to doubt that I have arrived at a sensible explanation for the woman's rather extraordinary antics shown on the disc. Now, do you want me to finished my explanation or shall I leave the matter in your hands from here on? Just say.'

Superintendent O'Hare decided it was time for a peace-keeping intervention. 'Please continue, Edgar. We all want to hear you out.'

Hodgkiss resumed after a hard look at Donald. 'Now, the question I posed before I was interrupted was this: why would Ms Bly not have spoken Berger's name when she had spoken the names of all the others on the list I gave Felix?

'I believe there is a sensible explanation and it is simply this; there was no need to say his name because she was speaking directly to him. He was standing before her, not three metres away.'

'Oh but that's nonsense Dad,' said Donald, his confidence waning noticeably.

'Not at all. If I'm talking to you on a one-on-one basis I don't say your Christian name and you don't say mine. It's not necessary. We now who we are.'

'If that's true,' said Donald, 'and I don't say it is, but if it is, then what was it all about …,what was she hoping to achieve?'

'Felix has already told us … she was trying to persuade Berger to come into the room. That is quite clear from some of her gestures. And the reason she wanted him to come in range of the camera was she intended to implicate him … set him up … frame him for Wisdom's death.

'Remember, the Bergers had a strong motive to get rid of Wisdom. He had turned them out of their three coffee shops … ruined them. And in addition he had made overtures of a sexual nature to Mrs Berger in most distressing circumstances.

'And tossing the belt she'd just used to strangle Wisdom in Berger's direction, and at such a height that he'd be certain to catch it, confirms that. She wanted his fingerprints on top of hers.'

Hodgkiss had just paused for dramatic effect when Esme put her head around the door. 'Sergeant Sanderson has just driven up. Will I send him straight in?'

'Yes, please Esme,' said the superintendent. 'Well, I wonder what news he's got.'

'If he's persuaded Berger to come with him he could clear up a lot of this speculation,' said Hodgkiss.

'I'm glad to hear you admit it's speculation,' said Donald. 'That's what I've been saying all along.'

'Yes, I agree it may be only speculation,' said the superintendent, 'but it's very likely accurate speculation. Berger certainly had motive to kill the fellow, Ms Bly knew that, and I think Edgar's right when he says she was trying to lure him into the room. I've seen that video a dozen times and it's always looked that way to me, right from the start. And the way she tossed the belt in his direction ... so he'd be sure to catch it. It had to be him out there because now we know he had the belt in his possession.'

Sergeant Sanderson was hovering in the doorway, a large file or papers under one arm.

'Come on in, sergeant,' the superintendent called. 'Come in and tell us what you found out from that Berger fellah. We've all got questions that need answers and they might be in those papers you've got there'

Donald asked. 'You didn't manage to persuade him to come with you. Pity. I wanted to get my hands on him.'

Sanderson nodded 'Yes. I think he knew that and that's

why he decided not to come. But he made a statement to me about what happened.'

'Excellent,' said Hodgkiss. He continued hastily 'But to spare you the trouble of reading it out, did he tell you why he went to Wisdom's unit that morning?'

'Yes, he did and I didn't have to ask him. He went to the unit because she ... Ms Bly ... rang him and told him to get over there ASAP. That she had some very good news for him.'

'About his coffee shops, no doubt,' said Hodgkiss.

'Yes. She told him that she'd persuaded Wisdom to let him stay on but that he'd have to sign some papers straight away. That's how she got him to go there. But of course as soon as he saw Wisdom lying dead just inside the bedroom door, and when she tried to persuade him to go into the room ...'

Hodgkiss nodded. 'Yes I can imagine He smelled a rat. He wasn't having any of it. And the belt? Where's that?'

'I left it in the kitchen with Mrs Burke. It's in an evidence bag. He said when she tossed it at him he'd caught it ... just a reflex action. Then too late he realised that his prints would be on it. He thought about burning it, but decided that we'd probably find it anyway and then he'd look guiltier than ever. So he decided he'd keep it and tell us what happened and hope for the best.'

'A very sensible man,' said Hodgkiss. 'His trust in the police process should be rewarded.' He turned to Donald. 'Not still hell-bent on arresting him, are you?'

Donald frowned 'Maybe not just yet. But he's still got a

lot of questions to answer.'

It was the best comeback he could think of at such short notice.

* * *

'Sergeant, normally I respect your slavish adherence to speed limits, but surely here, with not another car in sight, it is hardly necessary.'

Sergeant Sanderson shook his head. 'Rules are rules, Mr Hodgkiss, and speed limits were made for everyone ... and for good reason.'

Hodgkiss recognised the futility of arguing.

There was much about the sergeant that Hodgkiss admired and even those traits which he deplored he could recognise in himself, so he did not pursue the matter.

He sat back and watched the gum trees go by.

Then the sergeant turned to him and asked. 'Have you decided yet what to do about ... you-know?'

Yes, he knew what the sergeant was asking, and yes, he had decided what to do about it ... the jewellery Nola and Gordon Stacey had stolen from the late Mrs Phyllis Connaught.

But there were complications. First, James Connaught had refused to press charges against the Traceys. He knew that his wife's death had saved him from certain financial ruin because of her gambling habits, and he had a sense of guilt about the physical injuries she had inflicted on the highly desirable Nola Tracey during the course of the burglary.

Yet he felt it unjust that the Traceys should benefit from his loss. This was confused by the fact that the insurance company had offered him a handsome payout.

So he had spoken to the sergeant and that Hodgkiss fellow about the matter, stating his position and his reservations. They had seemed to understand and he had agreed to leave the matter in their hands as long as any solution did not affect his position vis-a-vis the insurance company.

Inspector Burke had been quick to wash his hands of the affair as soon as he refused to pursue charges against the Traceys. The inspector had told him if he wanted any further advice he should consult the Sergeant Sanderson who now had sole carriage of the matter.

So when Sergeant Sanderson asked if Hodgkiss had decided what to do about the problem, Hodgkiss declined to answer in the affirmative because although he had in mind an outline of a solution he held back; there was still some work to be done ... there were Is to be dotted and Tees to be crossed.

Ten minutes later Hodgkiss glanced at his watch and made a swift calculation. At the present rate of progress, if you could call it that, they would arrive at the Buccaneers' Bay Cruising Club in twenty minutes ... exactly twenty minutes late.

He could imagine Nola Tracey pacing impatiently on the front verandah of the clubhouse.

In this Hodgkiss was mistaken. Nola Tracey and her husband, Gordon, were sitting in the club bar, with the barman, Albert, setting down drinks in front of them.

Gordon picked up his beer, took a gulp, smacked his lips and set it down again. 'Don't forget to take them off before they get here,' he said.

Nola raised a hand to the string of large baroque pearls around her neck. They were totally out of place with the top she wore, with shoulders cut out to show the smooth brown skin of her upper arms.

'I'll take them off that stuffed shirt inspector decided to come along with them, otherwise they stay right where they are,' she said, then added, 'and Hodgkiss said he'd do his best to talk him out of it. Apart from him it hardly matters who sees them.'

'I'm not a pearls man,' said Albert. 'Normally I think of pearls on a par with ball bearings ... hard and shiny. But I make an exception for them They seem to glow ... from the inside.'

'And that too,' said Gordon, dropping his eyes to the large gold chain that hung around his wife's neck, the end disappearing between her breasts. 'That'll have to come off too.'

Nola shook her head 'Same thing ...only if *he* comes ... Burke. Otherwise they stay right where they are.'

'But even if he's not there there'll be that other copper ... the sergeant. We can't let him see them. He knows what happened ... he'll know where they came from.'

'Don't worry about him. He's a pussy. Besides, Hodgkiss will know what to do with him.'

'Sometimes I think you expect a bit too much from Hodgkiss. He can't work miracles, you know.'

'Well don't tell him that ... not before he's worked one or two for me.'

She slid gracefully down from the high stool. 'I suppose I should go out front and be ready to play hostess and sign then in. Hodgkiss warned me that if Burke didn't come and the sergeant was driving they'd be late. Well, they're late now so I think we can assume Burke's not with them.'

When the clubhouse came in sight Sergeant Sanderson turned to his passenger. 'I think you said something about Mr Tracy taking us out on his boat. Is that still on?'

Hodgkiss nodded. 'Yes. I believe that's what they have in mind. A day on the river, he said.'

'"A day on the river," the sergeant repeated. 'Like the Connaughts,' he said, unsmiling.

'I hope not,' said Hodgkiss.

Minutes passed. 'Esme wasn't exactly pleased with the way we handled it, you know.' Hodgkiss said.

'"Not pleased? Why? What did we do that ...' The sergeant raised a hand from the steering wheel to strike his forehead. 'Of course. The spotlight you mean. Not enough for the inspector.'

'Apparently not,' said Hodgkiss. 'He complained about it in bed last night. My room's just across the hall and I could hear him going on about something. I assumed it was that and thought about getting up and putting our side, but I thought it best to leave it up to Esme ... if she wants to say anything.'

'But it wasn't easy to give him any credit when he was being so negative about what we'd done ... particularly about Felix and what he'd done.'

'Exactly,' said Hodgkiss. 'I think Esme understands. She hasn't said anything... yet. And any word on Ms Bly?'

'You know we found her and charged her. Well, she's skipped bail. She could be out of the country by now. I suppose there's nothing much to keep her here now.'

'She didn't inherit anything then?' Hodgkiss asked.

Sergeant Sanderson shook his head. ' I saw that solicitor again and it turns out Wisdom never wrote a will, not so far as he knows anyway. He thought Wisdom might have had that girl prepare one for him. That's why he suggested we ask her. If she did we haven't found it yet. I suppose she might have taken it with her ... where ever she's gone.'

Five minutes later the sergeant slowed the car and swung into the club's empty parking lot. 'Here we are,' he announced unnecessarily.

Hodgkiss nodded through the windscreen. 'And there *they* are ... our welcoming committee. The Traceys ... Gordon and Nola ... a very pleasant couple.'

'Easy on the eye ... the lady in particular. Interesting, I'd call them. An interesting couple.'

'Yes, certainly interesting. What are you like on a boat? Not subject to *mal de mer*?'

'Not on the river, I shouldn't think,' said the sergeant, applying the handbrake. 'They're not thinking of putting to sea, are they?'

'I've no idea,' said Hodgkiss. 'Why? Is it a problem?'

Sergeant Sanderson shook his head. 'No. But we'd be late getting back and the inspector wants to know what happened before the day's out.'

Hodgkiss looked up, surprised. 'He didn't say anything to me about a report.'

'He doesn't want a report ... not a report as such. He just wants to know what you ... what we decided to do about ... everything.'

'I see. Doesn't trust us. Is that it?'

'I don't think it's that, really. I think he's just interested to hear what we ... what *you* do about it ... how you sort it out. And to be perfectly honest, so am I.'

Hodgkiss shook his head slowly. Yes, he thought. I'll be interested to know how I sort it out too ... how things will turn out ... *if* they turn out. There were still so many ifs.

Then Nola was at the window beside him.

She pulled the door open. 'No Inspector Burke, then?'

'You're always business, aren't you ... eye on the ball,' said Hodgkiss climbing out and planting a kiss on Nola's cheek.

'A girl's got to protect her interests.'

'And her assets.'

'Yes. Them too,' she said taking his hand and leading him toward the veranda where Gordon was waiting.

'Ah, the signing-in ceremony,' said Hodgkiss. 'We must

preserve the proper forms.'

'No, not today, Edgar. We promised you a day on the river and a day on the river you shall have.' She turned to Sanderson. 'Both of you. It's a perfect day for it, so why waste time indoors. We've got a substantial and healthy lunch, with alcohol, already packed and stowed on board, so instead of wasting time at the bar we propose taking to the water straight away. All in favour please say Aye. We can drop anchor somewhere along the way and eat.'

'And drink,' Hodgkiss added. 'But before we go ... a word in your ear. There are still one or two details you and I must resolve before we set sail ... or diesel or whatever one says.'

So Hodgkiss and Nola Tracey walked away a short distance to the side of the clubhouse and spoke together quietly but earnestly. Occasionally Nola raised a hand as if in protest at some proposition of Hodgkiss', but after a few more words it seemed her objections were over-ridden.

Soon the two returned to the veranda where Gordon and Sergeant Sanderson stood making awkward conversation.

'Ready to go now, are we?' Gordon asked with determined cheerfulness.

'You go ahead,' said Nola. 'I have to fetch something from my locker. I'll see you on board in a minute or two.'

Hodgkiss and the sergeant were standing barefooted on the back deck of the Trident when Nola appeared around the corner of the clubhouse, carrying a small silver box.

She put the box down on the deck of the marina and began to remove her sandshoes.

Hodgkiss asked 'How are your soles healing?'

'Nearly better,' she said. 'I've always been a quick healer, thank goodness. But you were right about the prints coming back. Scraping them off wouldn't have saved me. Much pain for no gain. I should have asked Doctor Google and spared myself the pain.'

She tossed her sandshoes onto the trident's deck then climbed aboard, clutching the silver box.

'And there's something else I'd like to know ... that is if either of you gentlemen is at liberty too tell me,' she asked.

'Ask away,' said Hodgkiss, 'although we may not be in a position to answer.'

'I think you'll be able to answer at this stage of the game. All I want to know is does Inspector Burke still think I murdered either of those people? I know that's what he thought last time I spoke to him.'

'Well of course I can't answer for Donald, but I can tell you that Felix, the lip reader, and I made it patently clear in our detailed report to Donald and the superintendent that Phyllis Connaught's death was certainly not directly attributable to Gordon and yourself, but to those who moved and dropped her.

'And as to who was responsible for Wisdom's death; we dealt with Ms Bly's role in that matter in quite emphatic and unambiguous terms.'

'Possibly a little too emphatic,' said Sergeant Sanderson, 'because after I delivered the report I looked into the inspector's office to ask if he had any queries. He was hunting through a dictionary, so I didn't disturb him.'

'"Hunting through a dictionary," Hodgkiss exclaimed. 'Why on earth would he have been doing that. Our statement about Ms Bly's guilt was concise and abundantly clear. As I recall we referred to her monologue in the bedroom and pointed out how that alone was enough to incriminate her. We summarized it with something along the lines; "the gravamen of Ms Bly's diatribe was basically exculpatory and therefore scarcely credible". No need for a dictionary there. All good English words.'

He turned to Nola and nodded towards the silver box. 'And those are ... the items?' he asked quietly.

'Yes. The items,' she repeated.

'All of them?'

'Yes. All ... as agreed.'

'Good. I'm sorry it has to be this way, but ... well, we don't want to go through all that again, do we?'

Nola sighed. 'No. No point ... unless you're about to change your mind.' Then hopefully. 'Any chance at all?'

Again Hodgkiss shook his head. 'You know my thoughts on the matter. I thought we'd agreed on this.'

Nola lifted her face defiantly. 'You should have been here the day we took them out. You'd understand then. She was an utter bitch. She did everything she could think of to put us down ... to put us in our place. And all that jewellery ... she wore it on purpose ... she had to. It was just another way to humiliate us. Not just me. Gordon too because he couldn't afford to buy me stuff like that. And all the time

Gordon was working for James' father for peanuts. I was provoked. She challenged me to come and steal the stuff.'

'I'd agree it was provocation … but a challenge for theft? Hardly. Besides, you know my thoughts on your conduct; it was not avarice … it was revenge. And Donald agreed although he took some persuading. Otherwise it wouldn't be happening like this. I promise you'll feel better about it when it's done.'

He paused then went on. 'Now, this is just a formality, but Inspector Burke will want a report when we get back. Obviously he will not be satisfied unless Sergeant Sanderson has viewed the contents of your little silver box.'

'By all means, Edgar,' said Nola. She picked up the box and handed it to the sergeant. 'Be my guest.'

Sergeant Sanderson took the box and raised the lid with some difficulty. He cast a cursory eye over the contents.

'Thank you, Ms Tracey,' he said. He closed the box and handed it back.

The big motor beneath the deck rumbled into strident life and Nola came quickly to her feet. 'Time to cast off,' she said and skipped nimbly around the cabin towards the bows.

Gordon came up from below deck and took the wheel. He edged the Trident away from the marina, turned and headed for the main channel of the river.

As soon as they were well underway Gordon began what Hodgkiss suspected was a well-rehearsed commentary on many of the prominent houses along the riverfront, together with details of their owners' personal histories.

They had been travelling only a short while when Gordon paused his commentary and turned to Nola. 'About here. This is the deepest part in this stretch of the river.'

Nola reached down, picked up the silver box, which was resting on the deck between her bare feet, and dropped it over the side.

Hodgkiss and Sergeant Sanderson leaned over to watch as the box sank quickly, in a straight line, out of sight.

'Done,' Nola said softly, then she took the esky from under the seat. 'Who's ready to eat?'

Glancing over the side, where the box had disappeared, Hodgkiss said: 'I thought that might have ruined your appetite. Apparently not.'

'It takes more than that,' said Gordon, reaching for a salmon sandwich.

They had no sooner finished eating when Sanderson's phone rang. He glanced at the screen. 'It's the inspector,' he announced uneasily then opened the connection and listened. 'Yes, Inspector, it's done. Just now. I saw it sink. Deepest part of the river.' A short pause. 'Yes, of course I did.' He listened again, frowning, then he glanced anxiously towards Hodgkiss. 'Yes, I believe so. There was a number of items in it, but of course I didn't have a copy of the inventory with me, so I couldn't say for certain. Yes. I'll do that.'

He cut the connection with obvious relief.

'Well done, sergeant,' said Hodgkiss. He turned to Nola. 'And those two very expensive-looking necklaces you were wearing when we arrived. What became of them?

'Both in the box, Edgar,' she said. 'At the bottom of the river.'

Hodgkiss turned to Sanderson for confirmation.

Sanderson looked the other way.

Hodgkiss smiled. 'Excellent. Then it's case closed. I'm sure we'll be able to hose Donald down if he gets fractious. Now, is there another one of those delicious little salmon tarts?'

Nola pushed the esky in Hodgkiss' direction. 'Help yourself, Edgar. And you were right … I feel much better about it already.'

❡

www.ingramcontent.com/pod-product-compliance
Lightning Source LLC
Chambersburg PA
CBHW020405120726
47904CB00002B/719